I0761533

◌ Praise for *The Glass Garden* ◌

"*The Glass Garden* is a sensual, despairing, beautiful hallucination, and Jessica Lévai crafts the lines of the tale with a disturbingly unerring precision. This is an elegantly crafted narrative with black-hole patience, each line as inevitable as the one that preceded it, drawing—as all the best tales do—to the only possible conclusion. A glistening, gloriously messed-up ride."

—Greg Rucka, writer of *Lazarus*

"A real sense of adventure and wonder, a fully realized world with history and mysteries we get a glimpse into, and incredibly deep, tender, and heartbreaking moments of a sibling relationship. Not to mention how visually stunning many of the scenes are, and that ending's gonna leave you wrecked. That, and a lot more, is what you have to look forward to from Lévai's newest SF/horror novella, *The Glass Garden*. It's nothing short of mesmerizing."

—Alex Woodroe, editor and cofounder of Tenebrous Press, author of *Whisperwood*

"*The Glass Garden* is a master class in dread-inducing. With her whip-smart prose and pitch-perfect dialogue, Lévai had me firmly on her hook from the book's opening lines. And the hook only sank deeper with every unsettling page thereafter. This is storytelling at its finest."

—George "Book Monster" Ranson

"Beautiful, lush, botanic space horror! Sublime, inexplicable terror! Seriously, read Jessica Lévai's *The Glass Garden*: it left me with a sense of wonder and terror unlike any other book I've read this year."

—Charlie Allison, author of *No Harmless Power: The Life and Times of the Ukrainian Anarchist Nestor Makhno*

THE GLASS GARDEN

THE GLASS GARDEN

BY JESSICA LÉVAI

LANTERNFISH PRESS

PHILADELPHIA, PA

THE GLASS GARDEN

Lanternfish Press
PO Box 34569
Philadelphia, PA 19101
lanternfishpress.com

Cover Design by Kimberly Glyder
Cover Image by Susan Wilkinson
Interior Layout and Typesetting by Hadley Hendrix

Printed in the United States of America

Library of Congress Control Number: 2024949540
Print ISBN: 9781941360873
Digital ISBN: 9781941360880

FOR LANNY, RAMADAN, AND ALICE

CONTENTS

DAY ONE

At least there was coffee. And it was glorious.

Therese sat in a hard plastic chair in the ship's galley, space-lagged and muzzy, contemplating a breakfast of packaged rolls and reconstituted eggs. It reminded her instantly of that years-ago winter dig in Gizeh. The first week, when the archaeologists were there alone, before the housekeeper arrived to take care of them properly.

But even the brilliant housekeeper in Egypt had never produced a cup like this. Therese let the steam envelop her, savoring the aroma before the next delicious sip.

Therese had landed planetside with her sister and one of her sister's crew members eight hours ago, in the jumpship of the *Maris Stella*. As they landed, they docked with the main ship, a small freighter in acceptable shape. For Lissy this sort of thing was normal, but for all that humanity had progressed in its exploration of worlds beyond the solar system, Therese remained a homebody. This was her first trip off world in over a decade.

Upon arrival, she had just enough time to dump her stuff in her room and collapse into bed to sleep off the jarring effects of space travel. She was still getting used to the gravity of the new planet, which her sister's freighter could not completely mitigate despite its excellent environmental controls. There hadn't been enough time for more than a glancing meet with the other members of the crew. Certainly not enough time to get a brief on how the hell she fit into the mission here. She even struggled to remember the designation of the planet they were on, though Lissy had told her several times.

Therese was accustomed to having weeks, if not months, of prep time before going on site anywhere. In addition to managing practical concerns, that time let her figure out who on the team was worth sticking to and whom to avoid. This was completely different. When she wasn't remembering the Gizeh dig, she had flashes of the first day of sophomore year, sitting in the cafeteria of a new high school knowing absolutely nobody, hoping someone would sit with her, terrified that they would.

"Fine brew as always. McArdle, you are the master." This was Eli Carver, the most recent addition to Lissy's crew, familiar to Therese from the jumpship and some casual conversation. Carver was handsome in a way that was easy to take in but not glamorous. You could look comfortably at him for hours if you had to, and his voice was smooth enough to make anything he said agreeable. His primary function in the crew, not that Lissy had said it out loud, was dazzling local bureaucrats of any gender to encourage their speedy processing of various licenses and permits, and he was good at it.

He sipped again at his mug and made a face of the most exaggerated pleasure before finding his way to a chair at the table with the rest of the crew, scone in hand.

"Someone has to be," Dana McArdle replied, their red curls glinting in the harsh light. It was the only real color in this drab, workaday room on a workaday ship. They were the pilot, the mechanic, and the first one consulted on the value of mechanical salvage. "Don't think the sweet talk is going to get you out of cleaning the machine. And properly this time."

Carver's smile grew less exaggerated and less genuine. "Aye, aye." His gaze fell on Therese over the cup in his hands. His eyes warmed up again as he asked, "Isn't this the best coffee you've ever had in your life?"

Therese took another sip to hide the smile that crept onto her face. "It is. McArdle, you made this?"

McArdle peered at Therese like she was some sort of bug. "I make all the machines run on this boat. Coffee press is no exception."

"They're being modest," said the dark-haired man sitting next to McArdle on their right, taking their hand. McArdle squeezed it back.

"They're really not," Carver whispered, leaning closer to Therese, two legs of his chair rearing perilously into the air. "McArdle cannot survive without good coffee, and they brought the press themself to make sure that we were always well-supplied. They're a coffee snob, if you can believe it." The chair legs clacked back into position as Carver rejoined McArdle and the other man. Tsieh, that was his name. Daniel Tsieh. Lissy had made a big production of listing his degrees and work experience. Back in her apartment on Earth, that had made Therese hopeful he would be something of a kindred spirit, but he barely made eye contact with her—just concentrated on his breakfast and on banter coded by experience and intimacy with McArdle and Carver. Therese took a deep breath and decided to distract herself from the feeling of isolation by slipping into anthropology mode, observing the human pond life with an eye to learning what made it go, and where she might fit in as this mission/expedition got going.

"Morning all!" called Lissy, splashing into the pond with all the subtlety of a rock thrown by a kindergartner. She poured herself a cup of coffee and drank what looked like half of it immediately. Hot liquid had never slowed Lissy down, to Therese's recollection. Lissy nodded and gave a thumbs-up to McArdle, who saluted with obvious satisfaction. Lissy looked from one crew member to the next, doing silent check-ins that spoke of familiarity, trust, and friendship. Only when she got to Therese did she speak aloud. "T, you good? Was your room all right? Get some food?"

"I'm all set," Therese answered. "Enjoying the coffee."

"Well, enjoy it fast, because we're going on site today, and I don't want to be late."

"Hold your horses, Captain," said McArdle. Therese observed how the title made Lissy's eyes light up. Lissy liked titles.

"It's not like we have a deadline, unless you have a buyer lined up you didn't tell us about."

"Yeah," Tsieh chimed in. "You gonna brief us, or what? What are we doing on this rock?"

So the crew didn't know what was going on, with the obvious exception of Carver. He had been there when Lissy made her impassioned plea to Therese, begging her sister to join them and appealing to her particular skills. Therese perked up a little at the idea of being even a little ahead of the rest of the people in this room, who clearly didn't understand how this job was different, but worried at the same time that it would give them a reason to hate her. Should she say something?

But Lissy didn't break eye contact with her sister, grinning around a bite of scone as if there was some great secret between the two of them that she alone would have the privilege of revealing. Washing down the dense pastry with the other half of her coffee, she plonked the mug down and sat on the table next to it, causing Therese to slide her own plate and mug away for safety. Lissy wiped crumbs from her mouth and addressed her captive audience.

"First off, gang, you've all had a chance to say hi to my big sister Therese, right?" Limp waves were exchanged. Carver smiled brightly, Tsieh a little less brightly, while McArdle sipped their coffee in silence. "T is on loan from Penrose University back on the home world, very prestigious, and we're all grateful she could make time in her schedule of teaching and publishing and whatnot to help us out with this."

Don't clap, thought Therese as hard as she could, wishing she could crawl into her cup. When no one clapped, she looked over the rim. Was she expected to make a speech? But Lissy continued.

"I know you're wondering why I decided today was bring-your-sister-to-work day, and here it is. This is not going to be our usual kind of job. This one is special." Lissy scooted off the table, pulling her device from a pocket. "I know I said, after the last time, that we were going to get a few months split up for much-needed R&R. But you all know me. My mind doesn't sleep, and I'm always looking out for us." She swiped at her device and began reading from notes. "What we have here is your standard abandoned mining colony, with some minor agriculture. Obviously nothing that panned out, or we wouldn't be here. We're going to scrounge up our usual tech salvage from the site, but this time we're also here for something a little more highbrow. I think we've found something with real archaeological significance."

Therese drank more coffee to drown a snort. Tsieh looked at Carver, who in turn was looking at Lissy with an expression of admiration and anxiety. This was getting interesting. Anthropologically, of course.

"What archaeology could there be with a colony? The oldest useful salvage we've found was what, fifty years old?" Tsieh asked. It was a fair point. Therese was about to chime in when he continued. "The older they are, the more stable, barring ecological disasters, so the stuff they leave behind isn't as valuable. There's no such thing as an ancient colony. What could possibly be so old or so interesting?"

Therese sat up a little taller. She knew what was coming; it had been the carrot Lissy dangled in front of her when she made her surprise visit to Penrose campus, showing up unannounced at Therese's apartment with the same entrepreneurial look on her face. Lissy knew her sister well enough to drop the real secret, the thing that would interest a professor when a regular salvage operation wouldn't.

"A previous civilization," Lissy answered, appreciating the muffled grunts of surprise from her crew. Therese nodded along. "Now, we all know that colonists are not as careful as they should be when they pick their planets. Nor as honest after the fact. Not all colonies are founded on the barren rocks they claim on the initial registration."

"Hold up," McArdle said, leaning forward. "Are we looking at something built on massacred indigenous? Because no. I'm not touching that."

"Easy, McArdle," said Carver. "I looked over the records with Lissy. There's nothing on file about that kind of thing, or really any intelligent state-building life. Just a smattering of micro- and megafauna, the latter of which come out at night and do not look like anything we want to meet in person. When we made our initial survey, we didn't see any evidence of violence. There aren't bodies or weird cemeteries. What we did see was . . . " Carver broke off, his eyes widening as if to swallow the room, but only for a second. "Sorry, Captain. It's your news."

"Thanks, man." Lissy rested her hand on Carver's shoulder for long enough that the gesture drew the eyes of everyone else in the room. "I swear, I'm not dragging us into any kind of conflict zone. The colony lasted twenty years, give or take. Communications show no unrest, no desperate requests for aid or weapons, just the usual bitching about veins not giving what they want, resources drying up, and shitty food. The kind of stuff that sends people packing, and they packed. But they left behind something amazing. So amazing, I'm going to bet they didn't make it themselves."

"So what is it?" Therese said. Everyone in the ship's kitchen faced her now. "You told me it was an artifact, but what are we specifically looking at?"

Lissy's mouth folded into that smug grin of hers. "I'd rather show than tell. So finish your breakfast already, visit the potties, and let's move out. Tsieh, you double-checked the air?"

"It's safe, but it'll take some getting used to," Tsieh answered.

"Great. Everyone grab an extra bottle of air and a mask on the way out. And a light; night falls fast and black on this world, and you'll need it at noon where we're going. We leave in twenty, people. Carver, get the camera. See you at the door." Ignoring the questioning looks that followed her, Lissy dropped her mug in the sink and left the kitchen. There was an uneasy silence among those remaining, McArdle's eyebrows so high they almost touched their curls.

Carver sighed apologetically and moved to bus his cup. "You heard her. Let's move." McArdle stood up and walked briskly to the coffee press, where they poured themself another cup, glaring at Carver the whole time.

"How did we get the clearance to come here, if this is such an incredible find?" Tsieh asked him. "I imagine the permits were a nightmare."

Carver nodded. "We're good. Trust me, guys, you'll see why Lissy's so excited. It's . . . it's something incredible."

"Will it come with an incredible payday?" Tsieh asked,

cutting off McArdle, who was probably about to ask the same question. "We can't take any more duds."

"Would you trust me?" said Carver. Therese made a sour face, sure no one was looking at her. Carver's grin was the same as Lissy's, and it might have been her voice coming out of his mouth. It was eerie how Lissy's boyfriends became extensions of her.

Carver put his mug and plate in the sink and headed toward the door. Tsieh and McArdle showed no signs of moving. "Carver, wait up!" Therese called, feeling the eyes of the other two on her back as she dumped her cup and ducked after Carver into the hall.

He did wait up, welcoming Therese again aboard the ship. "It's really great that you agreed to come. I think you'll be glad you did," Carver said as he led her through the cramped halls. "When Lissy gets excited, well—I'm sure you know, as her big sister. It's infectious."

"It's something all right."

"Good to have you on the team, Dr. Blake."

Therese laughed. "Oh, please, don't call me that unless I'm grading you."

"Tracy, then? Or T?"

"No." That came out faster and louder than she thought it would. "Therese is just fine, Eli."

"We mostly do last names here among ourselves. So Carver, if you don't mind."

Therese squinted at the barrier that erected itself between them. Maybe she should have stuck with "Dr. Blake," but it was probably too late now. And Lissy complained whenever they were together that only complete idiots and pathologically insecure people insisted on being called "Doctor" for a humanities degree. Therese had no idea how deeply this idea had permeated the rest of the crew. "Except for Lissy?"

"Well Lissy is just . . . Lissy." They arrived at equipment storage and Carver pressed a button to open the door. "But it makes sense to use first names with two Blakes on board, right?"

He was dancing. Therese couldn't resist giving him an extra spin. "How long have you and she been together?"

He grinned. "A gentleman never tells. And neither do I. Here." He handed her a mask: a plastic and metal cup that fit over her face, nose to chin, with straps to hold it in place and a tube for connecting it to the bottle he handed her next. She turned the mask over in her hands, getting the orientation, and slipped it over her head and face with one motion. Carver whistled. "You've done this before."

"Not my first dig. There are some deep places on Earth you don't want to breathe in." Her voice sounded tinny in the mask. She checked the level on the air canister but didn't turn it on yet. "Is this a dig, Carver? I'd really like to know what I'm getting into."

Carver slung the mask around his neck, then reached onto an upper shelf for a camera. "Lissy was right. You worry too much." He put a hand on her upper arm. The warmth from his fingers reached her skin even through the tough fabric of her jumpsuit and left a cold patch when he drew away. The sensation ran deep and she forgot to be pissed off at his patronizing tone. "Let's go!"

The five of them lined up at the door of the airlock, wearing layers of clothing against what Lissy said was a brisk outside environment. To Therese, the group was the epitome of ragtag, which made sense for salvors. It was even romantic. She observed the small physical intimacies between Tsieh and McArdle and smiled beneath her mask. They were clearly a couple. Lissy was the leader, and Carver? They looked too closely at each other, finished one another's sentences, communicated without saying a word. Despite his demurring, she was sure the two of them had at least hooked up. Which left Therese the odd one out, wishing she and Dave had stayed together at least long enough to do this trip, so she wouldn't fall into the stereotyped gap of the older, sexless, eccentric professor. But Dave would probably have published her research under his name afterward, so really, it was for the best.

The airlock opened and the outside air hissed in, striking everyone's unprotected eyes with an acrid fug. Therese blinked against the tears that dripped onto her cheeks. The rest of the team was cursing but clearly used to this sort of thing. Once her vision was clear enough, she stepped down the ramp with the rest of them and took in the three-hundred-sixty-degree view of the planet's surface. It was desolate, desertlike, with not much to see besides rocks. Therese held a hand up to her face to shield her eyes from the weak blue light of the alien sun. With the ship at their back, a ridge of rock lay directly before them, toward which Lissy began leading the trek. Therese hoped their business was someplace before the ridge, since no one brought any equipment to climb it.

"A little faster, please," came Lissy's muffled voice through her mask. She was ahead of them by a few strides, Carver right behind; Tsieh and McArdle stood shoulder to shoulder behind him. Therese sheepishly brought up the rear. Catching up to the crew, she fell behind again soon, her training taking over. "What's the matter, slowpoke?" Lissy called.

"Survey!" she answered, squatting low to examine the dirt and rocks around her. "Looking for evidence of intelligent construction."

"Later, T, come on!" Lissy resumed the path toward the ridge.

Therese hustled to keep up. Why even bring me, she thought, if we're not going to do this right? Still, she kept her eyes on the ground, watching their boots form tracks in the powdery dirt. She swung her gaze from side to side, looking for anything that was too regular, too angular to be produced naturally. Perhaps this is why she missed that the crew had stopped, and banged her head into Carver's back.

"Sorry," she said. Carver only smiled.

"Okay, let's pause a sec," said Lissy. "The ridge about one hundred feet in front of us? It's a cave system. So we are going to go in together and . . . " Here she pushed the words extra hard in Therese's direction. "*Do not separate* until we have a better map of the insides. Get your lights ready, but be prepared to douse 'em on my say-so."

"Wait, Lissy," said Therese. "Where is the colony? I'm not finding markers anywhere."

"You wouldn't and you won't. Colony's remnants are in that direction." She flung her arm toward the ridge, indicating the land beyond it. "And we will hit that later, but the real meat is in the cave."

"Meat? Are there animals?" McArdle fiddled in their belt, where Therese expected to see a pistol. Only tools were visible. The other crew shifted. Was anyone armed? Should they be?

"Not even bones," said Lissy.

At this a dry wind picked up, whispering against the rocks and dunes, whistling through the gaps created by the tubes of Therese's breathing apparatus. She scanned her field of vision for movement. Some sort of flying creature, batlike, circled on the horizon. She listened for the friction of life against the ground, but the air canister pump was too loud. If there was anything alive on the surface, it seemed to be giving them a wide berth. But we're the aliens, aren't we? she thought. Intruding where we shouldn't.

Again the party had moved on without her. Therese jogged after them. The chemical smell of canned air was making her nostrils burn and she tilted her mask to the side to sample the planet's air for just a second. Musty and pungent, it sent her back into the mask. Even if they could breathe this atmosphere, they would need some sort of filter to keep from tearing up.

The mouth of the cave stood about four meters high, gaping and blacker than it should have been: a maw, not a plain rock formation. Therese trembled; the others shivered. She blamed the chilly air and hoped they did, too. The comradely banter had stopped, carried away by the wind, and now there was just this darkness in front of them. Even Lissy was quiet, her focus on the cave entrance and not on the faces of her companions, whose jaws dropped as far as the masks would allow, then closed for nervous swallows and licking of lips.

"Lights on," said Lissy. A few clicks from Therese and McArdle and Carver. Tsieh hadn't moved.

"We're going in there?" he asked.

"Well, duh," Lissy replied.

"Is it safe? Is it stable?"

"It's a cave that's stood here for decades, if not centuries. Sure, it's stable. There's a nice wide path and Carver and I didn't encounter any problems when we scouted. Come on, we've been in worse."

"Worse man-made structures, yeah, but at least . . . "

"Hey." Carver looked Tsieh in the eye. His voice was soothing, even to Therese's ears. "It's okay. It's more than okay. Trust me."

Whether the words or the tone, it seemed to work. Tsieh clicked his light on, and the five beams together struck the waiting mouth, dissolving into the dark.

Therese continued into the cave in survey mode, noting the angle of the light from outside, measuring the puddle of it on the floor before her. The rock walls glistened. Probably volcanic glass. The air was dry against her eyes, but not as dry as the air outside. The ground was smooth, nearly slick, and she placed her feet carefully.

Lissy's voice rang out. "Stay close behind me. There's a fork leading off to the right ahead. Don't take it; we'll come back to map it out later. For now, go straight." The crew obeyed, beams from their flashlights dancing in front of them. The narrow passage grew narrower, the ground bumpier. The swinging lights made Therese feel seasick. She reached for the wall to steady herself and nearly fell when her hand slid across the improbably smooth surface. More minutes passed; the sound of their footfalls echoed against the walls.

In time the roof of the cave lowered until everyone was forced to stoop down while walking. Therese shuddered and forced herself to take deep breaths to ward off her very specific claustrophobia. As long as she could stand up, she'd be fine, but this? Once she'd visited the inside of a pyramid with colleagues on their day off. As they stood in the central chamber, one started hyperventilating at the mere thought of the tons and tons of stone stacked above them. Therese didn't mind it at all. But the tunnel leading into the chamber, with its short roof and one naked bulb? That had been a challenge. This was worse. Many people in a small (unexplored) space? The ceiling so low they were forced to bend at the waist or crouch to pass? Therese shut her eyes and focused on the feel of the tunnel, until they were through and she could stand at almost full height again. It wasn't so bad. If it was over soon, it would be better.

Lissy raised a hand. "Okay, gang. We're here. Carver, you want to stay out here with the lights or come in?"

"I'm not going to miss this." The exchange resembled two five-year-olds ruining their mother's surprise party.

"Lights off, everyone," Lissy commanded.

Assorted grumbling dribbled around the face masks, but no lights went out. “We’ll be in the dark,” Tsieh said.

Therese sighed into her mask. “Lissy, what are you doing?”

Lissy swung her light over the cave ceiling until it shone in Therese’s face. “T, I promise, the drama you’re putting out is nothing next to what awaits you around the corner. Just turn off your lights already. And watch your step.”

“How are we supposed to do both?” McArdle complained, but turned their light off all the same. The others followed, including Therese, who now had bright motes floating in her field of vision and had to rub her eyes to clear them. What choice did she have? She’d come so far for this, whatever it was. When she opened her eyes, she saw the subtlest shift in the floor, a pale blue glow suffusing it. It seemed to come from the stones themselves.

“What?” gasped Tsieh.

“See? Trust me, and keep walking.”

How many steps of trust had the crew taken with Lissy? Therese wondered. More than she had, and they all led to this dark, alien place. Huddled together, feeling reassurance now from the physical presence of another person in front of her, Therese followed the crew. One step, then another. At least the ceiling was higher here. She could stand up and breathe, even if it was just the canned air. It calmed her. Another step, Lissy’s encouragement sinking into the slick walls.

The glow grew stronger. It was a muddy light, too many colors in one place but not enough to make it pure white. The glow scattered and broke against the shadows made by the party as they edged forward.

"Almost there."

The crew turned a corner ahead of her. Therese listened to their footsteps, shuffling together and then stopping entirely. She made the turn herself and was grateful for her mask. The air had gone out of her, and she wasn't sure the atmosphere of this planet was enough to bring it back.

She whispered the most eloquent word she could think of. "Shit."

The tunnel had opened into a vast cavern. Distance estimation had never been her strong suit, but based on the heights of those assembled, Therese guessed the ceiling was twenty meters high at the topmost point, sloping to half that where it met the walls. Tunnels led away on the opposite side, giving the impression that this was the focus of the whole cave system, a sort of central terminal. The walls were the same igneous black, bathed in the gentle light that had guided them here. It seeped in the crevices so there were few shadows. It was dramatic but not blinding.

Therese fiddled with the clasps on her mask. Eventually her fingers caught just so and she flipped the catches open. A thin stream of air crept in, cool against the trapped heat of her breath, shocking as she pulled the mask off completely. She shook her head, feeling the weight of her hair in its messy bun and her scalp damp with sweat. It was warmer in here than it was outside, the air moist and fresh. She looked around, guilty, ready to be snapped at for this breach of safety protocols. But Tsieh and McArdle were likewise removing their masks, and while Lissy kept hers on, her smile shone through the plastic and metal as clear as anything. "What did I tell you?" she said.

The wall, the window, the glow. In her head Therese came up with many names. It was unprofessional and none of them were adequate anyway, but she was driven by a desperate need to translate what she was seeing into language, into something familiar, tangible, understandable; this was none of those things. One wall of the cavern was lit as if from behind, and upon it were . . . images. Like a stained glass window in an abandoned cathedral, sunlight pouring in at just the right angle to throw color and shapes on the dark expanse of the floor. But here, only the glow itself projected down. None of the details.

But what details! Therese had seen plenty of stained glass in her day, but this was an order of magnitude finer. The leading (it couldn't be leading, not this thin) was like strokes of ink on paper. As she moved closer, she saw that the window (no, it wasn't a window—she needed a better word, a more accurate word, but what could be accurate here?) began about a meter off the ground and ended maybe three meters above her head. The images impressed on it reminded her of Tiffany lamps at the art museum, but more free, more alive.

It was a controlled explosion of what could only be called flowers on vines. She followed one, a stripe of powdery gray, to see where it led. It twisted among the flowers while a black branch of the same shape imitated it. A shadow? An evil twin? The flower on this vine had a bulbous calyx, spotted in red and white with veins that reminded her of an infected eye. Was she being watched? Spiky black flowers sprung from a purplish stem. Living or dead, she couldn't tell and wouldn't guess. Other flowers were unexpected shades of green, or grew tentacles where you expected petals, ringed in circles like boils.

The windows in cathedrals showed martyrs, clutching lilies or roses or whatever their iconography dictated. These were not those flowers. These were the flowers that watched martyrs put to death and grew exuberantly, mockingly, from their remains.

"My God." The prayer echoed and Therese saw that everyone's eyes were on her. She blushed, but McArdle nodded, and she knew her reaction was hardly hers alone.

Therese stepped a bit closer, to take in more detail. There were creatures among the flowers, too angular to look like any arthropod she'd ever seen on any world. They flew, they crawled, they came in as many sizes and shapes as the flowers. The wings were made of glass—not just in the wall, she felt certain, but in whatever real life forms inspired it. They resembled an insect's idea of a space shuttle, or vice versa. Alighting among the flowers, predator and prey, but Therese couldn't tell which was which. Having scrutinized the tiny lines of the wings, the wispy tendrils that emerged from the stamen of a lilac flower, Therese took three steps backwards to better see the image as a whole. The patterns before her were gorgeous, swirled and chaotic, life caught in glass, strands echoing and twisting with no beginning or end. It was transcendent.

Tsieh and McArdle remained glued to their position on the floor, except that now their shoulders were touching as they leaned together for support. Neither had spoken since entering the cave, but their eyes were wide. Lissy and Carver had now removed their masks and were beaming at the rest, their flesh picking up the bluish glow. Therese's heart thumped in her chest, but Lissy looked, well, like Lissy. Comfortable and calm in the middle of wonder or danger.

"So what do you think?" Lissy asked Therese, shaking her from the thoughts that had begun to swirl in her head, mimicking the splendor before her. It was pleasant to be distracted by beauty, especially in a place such as this.

Therese cleared her throat. "So, is it a light well?" she asked. "Illuminating it from behind?"

"Nope," Lissy answered. "Carver and I thought that too, when we saw it the first time, but we went over the range in the jumpship and there's no opening we could find. Later we'll get a drone or two to look closer, but it seems to be glowing by itself. The wall is glowing."

"Bioluminescence?" asked Tsieh. "I mean, a fungus could have created this pattern. Or maybe remnants from the flowers . . . " He trailed off.

"Does anything about this look alive to you?" asked McArdle. "It's a two-dimensional picture of flowers and bugs. Somebody made it."

"Life permanently fixed in homage to itself. An offering to beauty." Therese didn't notice the silence that greeted her words. She breathed in deep and detected a scent she couldn't quite pin down, like fresh grass or spices. She was closer to the image again, with no memory of walking. Carver stood next to her, the glow from the images turning his handsome face into something angelic. He seemed transfixed.

"It's amazing, wasn't I right?" he said to Therese. The twinkle in his eye faded and he returned his gaze to the wall. "It's almost like . . . " His fingertips swept across the images directly before him, seemingly in slow motion, but Therese couldn't bring herself to stop him.

"Carver, don't touch it!" Lissy burst between her sister and her crewmate, slapping his wrist away from the wall. She locked eyes with Therese and said, "We shouldn't get our fingerprints on stuff, right, T? We don't know if the oils in our skin could damage the artifact."

Therese had to shake her head for the logic to break through. "Yeah, absolutely." She took a closer look at the wall. "I don't think he hurt anything, though. Looks all right to me. We should be more careful going forward, especially since we don't know how fragile this is. Or even what it's made out of." Her voice trailed off into a sigh.

"Okay," said Lissy in her boss voice. "T, put your mask back on. I don't think you're used to the air yet. Carver, this isn't one of our regular trash hauls. Don't touch anything until she gives us the all-clear." Therese complied; her head was filling with fuzz. At least the mask only covered her nose and mouth, and not her eyes. She wasn't ready to give up this vision, not quite yet. It was the most alive thing she'd encountered yet on this trip. The most wild.

"Okay, Boss, we get it." McArdle's voice seemed softer, but that was probably the mask they'd replaced on their head. "This is incredible. Are you sure we can detach it, though? I'm not sure how we'd get it out of the cave."

Therese spun to face them. "We can't remove it! What are you talking about?"

"I'm talking about how removing things of value from dead sites is what we do. We're salvors, not curators. Unless you think we're going to settle down and start charging admission."

"It's priceless," Therese sputtered.

"Exactly," said Tsieh.

"Easy, all of you," said Lissy. Her face was still bare. "Don't give us the 'it belongs in a museum' speech, T. And don't disrespect my people." Therese's stomach dropped and she turned quickly to avoid McArdle's eyes. "But no," Lissy continued, loud enough for everyone to hear. "We are not going to hack it off the wall and ship it to some weirdo to store in his basement. This is a find, I think we all agree, and whatever happens to it, I want to make sure that we, all of us, get the credit and the money we deserve for finding it and doing the initial work. This is why I brought you here. We can handle equipment and the odd shiny thing, but you're the only person I know with the experience to handle something of this magnitude. So here's what we're going to do. We're going to head back to the ship, and we're going to make a plan. Therese is going to walk us through the steps to deal with this properly. Then, tomorrow, we get to work. That okay with everyone?"

There was a general grumble of assent. Lissy turned her light back on. It was harsh and yellow in the cave and Therese feared for the flowers and their delicate constitution, whatever it would prove to be. She wanted to protect the art, but she also didn't want to get yelled at. Lissy returned to the tunnel they'd entered from, Carver following close behind but looking over his shoulder. Tsieh and McArdle followed, and Therese too, filing out of the presence of the most wonderful thing any of them had ever seen.

Therese's feet kept pace better with the rest of the party on the way back to the ship, but her mind wouldn't stop racing, and she had to let it. This was how she did her best work.

That thing in the cave was art. It was stunning. It was maybe alive? What had she just seen? Who could have constructed such a thing, and where the hell did they go? Civilizations died all the time, she reminded herself. Climates changed, fires or famines happened, and you had no choice but to pack up and move what you could. Sometimes it wasn't enough; this planet had no intelligent life on it anymore. The same forces that doomed the window's creators had probably made life hell for the colonists, and no matter how gorgeous the rock art in the cave, it wasn't anything you could eat. Probably.

In between these speculations her thoughts aligned in straight rows, step by step, laying out everything they would have to do next. Surveying, recording. Chemical sampling and analysis. Did they even have the necessary equipment? It would be easy enough to obtain off world, but that would take time, and who wanted to take time with something so incredible?

Movement caught the corner of her eye. She squinted against the sun, now angled directly into her line of vision. About thirty yards away, two creatures were playing, or fighting. They had leathery wings, surprisingly beautiful; they resembled the flying predator she'd seen before. Seeing them closer sealed the identification. Every so often, one of them bounced up from the ground, snapping something in its sharp jaws, then returned for more. Therese walked toward them, slowly so as not to startle them, but that was a failure. The two creatures locked eyes on her, harmonized a sharp cry, and flew away to an outcropping of rock some meters away. Therese pursued them a bit further but stopped before her boot crushed what had been the object of their focus.

It was small and furred, another native of this planet, now dead and taking its next spin on the circle of life. The winged things had pulled it open, displaying its guts like an expensive carpet, strings and tubes of varying color and texture shining wetly in the blue sun. Therese crouched closer. Without a probe, or even a thin twig, she had to satisfy herself with mere visual inspection. She had glued together plenty of pots from sherds, reassembled cracked reliefs and sculptures, but something so alien and once alive was another story. She despaired of identifying the parts and it would make no difference if she could; dead is dead. It fascinated her nonetheless. A black hole where one of the eyes had been was rimmed in greenish blood, but the other eye remained, purple with black pupils slit in a complicated petal pattern. It looked like a jewel but for the film forming on it. She wondered what it would feel like to the touch. She reached out her hand.

"Sis, what the hell are you doing?"

Lissy's shadow slid over the beast's eye, robbing it of any shine. Therese sighed with the effort of standing up. Even through the mask, she could read the disgust on Lissy's face. "Do you study roadkill at home, too?"

"Sometimes," Therese answered honestly. "It's the only time I get to see wild animals up close, you know? Much less their insides."

"Okay, ew. We need to get to the ship so we can start processing the find. Remember? Why you're here?"

"Yeah, I'm coming."

"Good. Let the rooks enjoy their breakfast."

"They're not rooks."

"They sure look like rooks. Or bats, I guess, but it's daytime, so rooks."

"But . . . okay." It was pointless to argue, and while expedition protocols strongly discouraged randomly assigning Earth names to alien flora and fauna, it fit. "You know, in some places, rooks are bad luck."

"They sure were for whatever that fuzzy thing was." Lissy didn't even look back again as she spoke. Therese followed her to the waiting crew, listening to their footsteps in the sand, waiting to hear the dry rustle of wings; wishing the furry creature safe passage to whatever came next.

The crew stumbled into the ship like kids completely drained from the effort of playing in the snow. They slipped off their boots, hung their masks, and placed their air canisters to be refilled. After washing up, everyone headed by silent consensus to the galley. McArdle poured themself a half-cup of the cold coffee. Tsieh and Therese sat in their plastic chairs, staring at the walls. Therese's fingers twitched for pen and paper, while everything was fresh. Carver whispered encouragement to Lissy as she paced at the counter, waiting for everyone's attention. It didn't take long.

"What the fuck *was* that?" asked McArdle, summing up the mood of the room better than Therese could hope to.

Lissy stopped pacing and stared at the floor. "I figure you guys probably have questions, but we need to come up with a plan, and fast."

"No," said Therese, "We need to know why you brought us here. What brought *you* here. How did you find this thing, Lissy?"

Lissy nodded, still looking at the floor. When she brought her head up, it was to make eye contact with Carver, now standing behind the others at the table. He tipped his head to her with a serious expression and gave her a thumbs-up. Lissy took a deep breath and seated herself in the last empty chair. "Okay," she said. "T, you're right. You need the whole story, and a little backstory." Singled out again, Therese chose to say nothing. She rested her chin on her folded hands and waited for Lissy to begin. "About three months ago, the crew and I went on sabbatical."

McArdle cut in. "Sabbatical is our fancy code word from when business . . . slows down, and we need some time away from each other."

"I get that." And Therese did. She was on her own "sabbatical," but they didn't need the details.

"During my time off I got to thinking and, believe it or not, big sister, I thought of you. What would T do?" Lissy sniffed a tiny laugh. "I actually spent time digging through old registration records. You know, the kind that they never digitized. There are places where these things are on paper, in boxes, in basements. I got so many paper cuts. I figured that by aiming our sights at older stuff, we might find something someone had missed. Or something more interesting than outdated scraps of metal."

"Even older outdated scraps of metal?" McArdle's voice had an edge.

"So here's the story of the planet hosting us. I would have done this earlier, but lectures are boring and I didn't want to bury the lede." She pulled her device from her pocket and swiped through the information. She didn't activate the holo, so there was no way for the others to see what she was reading. "This planet, which has a long, tedious, number-and-letter-soup official name, but which we may more casually call Planet Paycheck, was first discovered about two hundred years ago. This was a completely remote affair at the time, long-distance telescopes, that sort of thing. I think T will back me up when I say that new planets are only explored to answer two questions. One—is there life? And two—are there exploitable resources?"

Therese nodded with a weak smile on her face. "You forgot three—will the life interfere with obtaining the resources?"

"Indeed. Well, once upon a time there were high hopes for question one. This was during that phase where any planet in the Goldilocks zone got intense attention, what with climate on Earth being an increasing shitshow. They graduated to probes and eventually discovered that there was life—you met some of it today, T, which was gross—but nothing advanced or intelligent. Most of the planet is what we see out our window. Dry and scrubby."

"Could we just once set down somewhere with amazing beaches?" asked McArdle. The rest of the room, Therese included, laughed.

"Beaches don't pay bills." The laughter died instantly. Lissy continued. "As for resources, nothing came up in the initial scans, so further exploration was put on hold for a while. A long while. There have been three subsequent attempts to colonize this world. The first doesn't come until almost a century after the planet is discovered, and they don't stay long. This is, mind you, on the other side of the planet. What records they left describe spacesickness, indigestible native flora and fauna, and erratic weather patterns. They hightail it out pretty quick.

"After that it's quiet for a while. Once private spaceflight becomes cheaper, we still don't see a lot of interest in this world. More probes, more disappointment. You know it's the pits when the next people to touch down are a religious colony. They landed here about fifty years ago. And by here, I mean just over the ridge from where we sit now."

"What kind of religious colony?" asked Therese.

"A weird one?" Clearly they had bumped against the limits of Lissy's knowledge.

Therese pressed on anyway. "Are they the ones who built that thing we saw?"

"I don't know. Maybe? If so, that's about the only trace of them. We don't know why they left. Unlike the commercial and scientific ventures, they wouldn't have been required to file flight plans or progress reports with an external agency. I found a pamphlet—an actual paper pamphlet—inviting people to join them, but we don't know how many did."

"So we have to reconstruct what happened based on whatever we find here." Therese pursed her lips. "Religious colonies almost never last. They've got more enthusiasm than know-how in most cases, plus a penchant for infighting. Still, no society vanishes without a trace. There's gotta be something they left behind, some documents, more art."

"If they're religious weirdos," said Tsieh, "they probably didn't leave behind anything for us to resell, though. I'm excited for the historical find or whatever, but what are we gonna salvage?"

"Don't disrespect the religious types," said McArdle. "They're responsible for a lot more exploration in history than you know."

"Yeah, and plenty of hoarded wealth, in some cases," Therese added. McArdle shot her a dirty look, and she blushed. She really needed to stop trying to be funny. "I take it there's more?"

Lissy scrolled through some more data. "After the cult, we have a regular old colony, the one I told you about. Right on top of the previous settlement. They landed, oh, fifteen years ago and lasted maybe five. They're the ones who are going to yield us the regular salvage, and I've no reason to think it won't be a decent payday. We're talking equipment, building materials, and electronics. Maybe even some easy-to-reach ore."

"Equipment's all gonna be old," said McArdle, shaking their head. "Weathered, too. Possibly no better than scrap."

"Well, after I did all my research, I got Carver to help me rent some kit. We did a flyby, and I don't think it's as bad as all that." Lissy sounded tired for a moment. It must be a lot, being so defensive all the time, Therese thought. Lissy shrugged off the uncertainty and said, "But come on, that wall, that window. It's amazing, isn't it?" Lissy looked from person to person, waiting for someone to validate her excitement. The room was stone still but for Carver's enthusiastic nod.

“How did you know that window was there?” Therese asked into the silence. “You couldn’t see that from a flyby.”

“You can see the cave mouth clear enough,” Carver replied. His mouth kinked upward. “I had a hunch about it. So I dared her.”

“We were looking for water sources,” Lissy cut in, shaking her head. “We knew the site was probably bigger than just the mining operation. We had to check.” A beat. “And yeah, there might have been a dare.”

These people have no idea what they’re doing, Therese told herself, and they don’t even know it. This is going to be a giant mess.

“Is it dangerous?” Tsieh asked.

“Well, if it were,” said Lissy, “this planet would be restricted, but it’s not. I checked it out. If we stay in the ship at night, I’m sure we’ll be fine.”

“I dunno,” said Tsieh. “Something about that window feels too weird.”

Therese had to agree. But weird or not, here they were. Lissy stole a sideways glance at her. It felt like a cry for help. She answered. “I will say that this is like nothing I’ve ever seen in my career. We’re really lucky the last colonists didn’t find it or damage it or exploit it. This is big. And . . . ” None of this was a lie. She was actually excited. “And I’m *here*. I’ve never been there for an actual discovery before.”

“I’m not stupid, you guys,” said Lissy. It felt like a pinch on the heart to Therese. “I know how bad the books are. I know that the last job was a disaster, and I’m not blind to the looks people give us rather than hiring our crew. But I have to believe that if we handle this right, this incredible thing, we'll come out ahead. Not just money, but honest-to-God respect. For all of us."

"Where do I fit in, on the money side?" Therese said. She spoke the words lightly, but all eyes focused on her, some more narrowed than others.

"I thought PhDs only got paid in publication offprints," said Tsieh. McArdle snorted.

Therese decided not to rise to the bait. "It will be a pretty sweet publication," she admitted. "But we do like to eat."

"Well, T, you're the ringer." Lissy's energy returned, her voice reaching that insufferable pitch. "Everyone pitches in, everyone gets a share. On that note, let's all turn our attention to our resident anthropologist/archaeologist, so we can come up with a plan for that window. Drawing. Whatever. What should we call it?"

"Nothing," said Therese. She ignored her sister's gaping mouth, rested her palms on the table and pressed the rest of her body to a standing position, but slowly. She wanted her thoughts to line up before she let them out. "We don't name anything without a real idea of what it is, and we don't know anything about this . . . thing. Not yet. We also don't know much about the context of where it was created, or even when. This is all information we need before we can proceed." The air was itchy with expectation, boredom, and Lissy's obvious determination to skip the hard work. "We need to survey. Survey and record everything."

"Duh," said Lissy. "We do that on all our jobs."

"Then you'll have the equipment." It was a snappish answer. Therese licked her lips, breathed deep through her nose, and said, “You have a drone? We need to get the lay of the land, see where the colony was, where the buildings were, what the traffic patterns were, as best we can. We can probably get a rough picture now, and fill it in with on-the-ground shoeleather work tomorrow. Who wants to handle creating a provisional site map?”

McArdle raised a hand. “I can do it. It’s usually my job, anyway.”

“And if you’re as good with a drone as you are with a coffee press, we’ll be in great shape.” It was sugar, it was saccharine, but McArdle seemed to accept it, the faintest smile curling their lips. “I want the timeline that Lissy and Carver compiled in a text form, something that we can all reference as we try to fit our findings into it. Can you get me that by tonight?”

“Yeah, sure,” said Carver, throwing a look over at Lissy, who was tapping her foot against a chair leg in the most annoying way possible. How did she not think this operation would require she take orders?

“What about the . . . thing?” Lissy asked, tapping a few more times for good measure. “I don’t know how long we’ll have this site to ourselves, and that’s the most valuable thing here. Valuable, I say before you start scolding me . . . ” Therese bit her lip to keep the reproach from flying. “Valuable in all the meanings of the word. Money, education, history human and not. When are we gonna get to that?”

Impatient, like so many of Therese’s students. Like Dave. “First we need to find out if it’s even safe. Have you tested for radiation? Airborne pathogens? Toxic off-gassing? Did you think of any of that stuff?”

Lissy's fingernails curled into claws against the table. "It's safe."

"Let's make sure. Do you have someone who can take and analyze samples?"

"I can," said Tsieh. "Lemme help McArdle with the mapping tonight, and I'm available for the samples whenever after that."

"Great. We also need to record it in every way possible. That means drawings and photographs, so—Carver?"

He was halfway to the door, but she'd caught him. "Yeah?"

"Photos? I think Lissy said that was your department?"

Carver looked at Lissy before answering. "Yeah, I guess that's something I can handle." He seemed confused. Therese took in his distant expression and bitten lip and decided that this might be his baseline.

"Cool. Get the photos to me as soon as you can." Therese stepped away from the table. "Everyone has their assignments, so I'll leave you to it."

"Wait." Therese stopped in her tracks, while Lissy approached her. "You said everyone had their assignments. What are you going to do while we're working?"

Therese felt herself shrinking away and actually grunted as she forced herself to meet Lissy's eyes. "I am going to start assembling a database of everything we know and identifying what we don't. That'll make what comes next a lot easier to figure out. Let's all meet up again . . . I dunno. When do you have lunch?"

"Given how short the days are, no lunch," said McArdle. "In four hours we'll have dinner. Three and a half, if you want to help assemble it." There was no question in those words.

"I'll be here," said Therese, easing around her sister and Carver on her way out. She didn't look back. Leaving a classroom, she never did.

Three and a half hours later on the dot saw Therese in the galley, where the rest of the crew was already rummaging in the cabinets, picking out assorted packets of food and prepping them. Therese slipped in as unobtrusively as she could, pulling cups from the cabinet where she'd seen them in the morning and setting them in a circle at the table. There were still only the four chairs, but she guessed they'd figure that out when the time came. She returned to the counter, where Carver had laid out a selection of fresh carrots, and helped herself to one.

"Those are mine!" he said, placing a hand protectively over the batch while Therese awkwardly chewed the bite she'd taken. "Sorry. It's just that I bring my own food on these trips. For when the processed stuff starts disagreeing with me."

"Let her have a carrot," said Lissy, squeezing goo-covered chunks from a metallic envelope into a bowl and popping it into the microwave. She turned to Therese. "You're okay with regular rations, right?"

"Sure," said Therese. "Standard issue on Earth digs too." Which wasn't true, but she wasn't going to be high-maintenance if she could help it.

"Carver's got weak digestion," said McArdle, peeling the plastic back from a tin of crackers and placing it ceremoniously in the center of the table amid the cups. "Real spacefarers learn to eat almost anything and keep it down. Or in. Whatever."

Carver stuck out his tongue at them.

"Ah, lay off," said Tsieh. "You've had your days." Tsieh brought a few cups of what Therese guessed were dips and arranged them around the crackers. "Okay, Therese, what do you want for a main? I'm afraid your sister took the last sweet-and-sour chicken."

"Fucking tattle-tale," Lissy muttered.

"But we got plenty of variety besides, allergens clearly marked." Tsieh led Therese to the cabinet and let her inspect the selection. She picked a box at random and waited for her turn to heat it.

Once everyone had settled down at the table, there was nothing but chewing and crunching for many minutes. Lissy chose to remain standing due to the chair shortage: between Therese and Carver, her arm intruding into their space every so often to grab food. One of the dips was a surprisingly fresh-tasting artichoke mix, and Therese had to steel herself not to inhale the whole thing. As for the boxed food, it was . . . adequate. She glanced at the others and figured they were of the same opinion. She'd better get used to it.

McArdle cleared their throat, wiped their mouth with a napkin, and said, "Let's check in. Tsieh and I will go first." They positioned their device before them and activated the holo so everyone could see. Lissy cleared the cracker remnants to the counter as the map appeared.

Therese shifted her chair to the other side of the table so

she wouldn't view things backwards. With her own device she took notes as the two explained where they'd scanned. Lissy chimed in with additions and corrections, and twenty minutes later they had a decent map, colony artifacts clearly marked. There was the footprint of a factory or refinery, probably, and some miles away the residential section where the colonists conducted business and slept. No agricultural markers. Various data indicated plenty of equipment to be salvaged—more, Lissy said, than she had been expecting. "Finally, some fucking luck."

"These are a big question mark, though," McArdle said, indicating some mounds near the refinery. "Are these natural or not? We couldn't tell from the air. We'll have to see when we go in."

"That's one problem," said Therese. "Here's another. All of this is beyond the ridge." Therese pointed out the jagged line on the map. "The colony would have been physically separated from the cave."

"What's your point?" asked Tsieh.

Therese was encouraged by his calm, non-judgy tone. "There just doesn't seem to be a connection, that's all. Also, it means we're working on two separate sites. We knew that, but it makes things a little more complicated. We could take them one at a time. You guys salvage what you can first, maybe even sell some of it, and then we come back to the cave and deal with it properly on its own."

"No," said Lissy. "No, we're doing the cave right away. That's the big thing. I don't want to risk someone else scooping us on it."

"It's riskier, though, isn't it, Boss?" said Tsieh.

“It’s why we’re here, and it’s why Therese is here, so we do it first. Or at the same time. But we don’t wait. So T, what do we need to do there? C’mon, I want a plan for tomorrow.”

Therese sighed and rubbed her eyes. The packet food she’d eaten would not give her the energy to fight. “Fine, here’s what I suggest. We split into teams. One team goes to the colony site and does survey on foot, recording everything. Probably take a couple of days. The other team gets started on the cave. Tsieh, you’re the one that’s good at chemical and electrical analysis, right?”

McArdle and Lissy simultaneously turned to look at Tsieh, who gave a resigned smile. “That would be me.”

“Okay, then Tsieh and I can take the cave. I want to do some sketches and measuring, too. Lissy, Carver, and McArdle handle the other site. While you were creating the map, I set up a database we can all access to store our reports.” This last part got the same wrinkled nose of disbelief from everyone else in the room. “Or just whatever we find. We have to document everything. Can I get your devices syncing with it? That’ll make things easier.” What followed was the sharing of contact codes and data and app packs, refreshingly familiar. The ship connected their devices, but communication with the rest of space was spotty. They needed each other and they needed centralized information. Therese always felt this step helped solidify colleagues as a team. Soon everyone had a copy.

“Hey, Carver,” said Therese, skimming the new data. “What happened to the photos? I don’t see ’em.”

“The photos?” Carver swallowed hard. “I didn’t actually get any. Any good ones.”

“Not even today? I thought you took the camera?”

"I did, but I was really, you know, distracted?"

Getting yelled at by Lissy would distract anyone. "Don't worry. I'll want to do it myself tomorrow, so I get what I need. It's okay."

"I can pack up the equipment tonight to get us started early tomorrow," said Tsieh. He reached behind his chair to the counter and came back with a small cardboard box. "After dessert," he said, tearing open the seal and distributing chocolate-chip cookies to everyone.

McArdle, Carver, and Tsieh gleefully left the sisters to kitchen duty. Therese didn't mind. She'd been hoping for a little more private time with Lissy anyway. Once the others left, Lissy reached far into a cabinet and drew out a tall black bottle. "Nightcap?" Therese smiled gratefully and pulled out two glasses. Lissy filled each with a finger of Irish cream. The taste was sweet and homey, not just because it came from Earth. "Remember when we used to sneak this, back in high school?"

"It helped that Mom hated it, so she never kept track of the liquid level in the bottle," Therese replied.

"I have a hunch that Aunt Jean kept giving her the stuff to keep us supplied on the sly."

"Aunt Jean was trouble that way, may she rest in peace." Therese licked the sweet stuff from her lips. "Speaking of hunches . . . this is an incredible find, Lissy. I know you know that."

"But . . . ?" Lissy's voice was guarded, and tired.

"I'm not patronizing you. I've never seen anything like that cave, ever, and I've dug up some weird shit."

"Weirder than hundreds of ceramic beer jars?" Lissy poured herself another drink, having downed the first one. She offered more to Therese, who held up a hand in polite refusal, then changed her mind and accepted.

"Beer jars are boring, not weird, and ugh, stop bringing that up. I've found other stuff. But seriously, what is in that cave? What is it meant to represent? I don't see any flowers at all around here. Maybe the planet used to be more temperate, and there was some sort of climate event? I guess whoever made it could have been remembering flowers from another world, and recreated them here."

"What about the bugs?" It could have been the alcohol making Lissy's voice higher. "They're unreal. Where did they come from?"

"The human imagination, you think?" Therese heard her own voice headed to the rafters and checked it. She'd forgotten how strong this stuff was, especially if you didn't find occasion to drink much and you were on another planet. "I mean, you're not gonna start like those morons who say aliens built the pyramids, just because the gods have animal heads. They don't have to be alien bugs in the first place."

"You suggested alien bugs, not me."

"No, I didn't." Forget it. The ship was a small house and there wasn't room for a fight. "I'm just saying, there is such a thing as imagination and creativity and the desire for something to be more beautiful and strange than life is, and also the desire to have the beautiful and strange completely under your control."

"You would know," Lissy muttered, though the words were clear enough.

"Come again?" Therese finished her own drink.

"Nothing." Lissy stifled a burp with the back of her hand. "I forgot how philosophical you get when you've had . . . half a drink."

"Oh, leave me alone, all right?" She knocked back the rest of her drink, for spite.

"I'm sorry." Lissy stared at the creamy ring left in her glass, then looked at her sister. "Thank you for coming on this trip. I really mean it. This is so important, and I want to get it right, and it's . . . nice to share living space with you again, just for a little while."

"What's family for?" Therese said, sincerity boosted by alcohol.

"What did the university say when you told them? What *did* you tell them, anyway?"

"The same thing I told Dave. I told them we were taking a break."

"Oh, man, that sucks. Dave, I mean. I thought you two were really solid."

"Yeah, I did too."

"Mom thought he was perfect."

Therese scowled. "She can date him, then. He was not perfect."

"Well, no one can be, if your standards are higher than . . . " Lissy shrugged. "Never mind. Forget Dave. Me, I always thought he was stuffy and pretentious."

"So what standards should I have?" Therese tilted her glass

against her lips, trying to get every drop. "Should I just hook up with whatever hot himbo comes into range?"

Lissy just looked at her. "Well." Lissy stood and grabbed Therese's glass, now empty, from her hand and put both of them into the sink, where they rattled against each other. "Since something crawled up your butt, that's my cue to leave. I'll wake you up tomorrow for breakfast and we can get started." Then she was gone.

Therese sat back in her chair and hissed a deep sigh. This kind of crap never happened on real excavations, where everyone was a trained professional who knew the rules of the job. Professionals for whom it wasn't just about grabbing shiny stuff and leaving. Professionals who, faced with small spaces and disparate personalities, knew to keep their mouths shut, seethe, and write blistering footnotes in their publications later.

Lissy tapped her fingernails in a complicated tattoo on the door, draping herself against the frame so she'd be in full view when Carver opened it. He stretched and yawned. "Evening, Captain," he said. He was wearing that cotton sleep set that hung off him so perfectly. Lissy couldn't help herself. She threw an arm around his neck and pulled him in for a deep kiss.

He broke it first. "Oof, hitting the Irish cream tonight, are we?"

"Don't start," she said, pushing past him gently and into the room. "Dose makes the poison, remember?"

"I wasn't gonna judge." Carver closed the door. When Lissy

flopped onto his bed, arms covering her eyes, he asked, "What did your sister do now?"

She let out a small, strangled scream. "She's just such a pain in the ass! It's like we can't be in the same space for five minutes without fighting like kids." Lissy sat up and crossed her legs. "You know, she broke up with her boyfriend."

"No kidding."

"For three years I had to hear about how wonderful he was, and how he was perfect for her, and now he's out of the picture. I guess even he couldn't live up to her impossible standards." Lissy watched Carver's eyes glaze over and was vaguely aware that not only was she boring him, but this conversation wasn't very fair to him in the first place. She chose a tactic to pull him in. "She said you were a himbo."

"A himbo?" The information seemed to hit him between the eyes and daze him. "That's the exact word she used?"

"Yep."

Carver went very still. "That's hilarious," he said in a flat tone. "Also really dated."

"Hey, don't worry about it," said Lissy. She reached for his hand, but he pulled away. "Therese doesn't like anyone who isn't published. She's always been like this."

"Yeah, well, if you hate her so much, why did you bring her on this job?"

Lissy felt a contraction in her throat and swallowed against it. "I don't hate her."

"She obviously stresses you out."

"Well, sure, but she's my big sister. That's her job. And she's the only expert I know on archaeology, and she's family, so she's someone I can trust."

"So, trust her." Carver put his hand on Lissy's shoulder. It was warm. He shifted to face her fully and she made herself listen extra hard because the way he turned displayed his chest so beautifully. "Trust her and let her do her job. Let us *all* do our jobs, and it'll work out fine."

She was almost lulled, but contrarianism was a trait she and Therese shared. "But she's so bossy! She's gonna make this *her* site, isn't she?"

"No, she won't. This is your job, Lissy. This is your discovery. You did all this work. She's gonna respect that."

"Ugh!" Lissy flopped away from him, onto her back. He was making sense and she was still too revved up to be interested in listening. "I don't want to talk about her. I just want . . . I don't know what I want."

Carver leaned over and stroked her cheek, then her lips. Her body awakened at the touch. "I think I know what you want," he said with a smirk.

"Yeah, I think you do," Lissy answered, and rolled over to reach for the light switch.

Therese didn't go to bed immediately, despite her brain fog. There was prep to do, if she was going into the cave tomorrow. A spike of adrenaline as she thought of the stained glass. No, not stained glass. At the most benign, calling it "stained glass"

would make it harder to come up with a different name or see it as anything but a human creation. It implied too much wishful thinking, even if the wish was only for understanding. She flicked on the holo of her device (much easier on her tired eyes than staring into the little screen) and thumped the end of her stylus against her lips in a thinking rhythm. It wasn't a window at all, not if no outside light came through. It glowed. Was there a term for a glowing mural? But no: *mural*, like *stained glass*, implied too strongly that humans or humanlike beings had constructed it. What if the glow was a form of bioluminescence? Bioluminescent creatures seemed likely enough. But creatures that could create art like humans did? She dropped her stylus. The click broke her from the spiral of thought. This was the wrong way to go about it. Everything had to start with agnostic documentation and testing. Naming would come later.

She wished she had pictures. Why didn't Carver take any? With a heavy sigh, she rooted around for a thick pad of paper and a pencil, the ancient tools of her trade and still a surprisingly up-to-date method. Flopping on her cot, she turned a fresh page in the notebook, smoothed the paper with her palm, shivered at the texture, and took up the pencil. She tested the sharpness of its point with the pad of her finger. It reminded her of the thorns. She shut her eyes a moment, steadied her breathing, and opened them to begin her sketch. The pencil danced lightly over the paper, then more heavily, as she sketched her memory of the . . . thing. The rough contours of the cavern appeared, a large empty area where the thing would be. She could add to it tomorrow, take real measurements, sketch in a map to be supplemented with detailed drawings. Like . . .

She turned a page quickly and shut her eyes again, focusing on the memory of the eyeball flower. The silver fly that flew over it. The sound of the pencil was soothing against the buzzing of a faulty overhead light and the constant hissing of the recirculated air system. When she opened her eyes, she had a drawing. Not a bad one, either.

She checked the ship's time, did calculations on a blank corner of her sketch. Definitely bedtime. Once she'd changed and brushed her teeth and hair, she slipped between the sheets of woven plastic material on the plastic cot and lay there like the world's cheapest, most boring action figure. Reaching over to the switch on the wall by her head, she killed the light and waited to see what would emerge from the darkness. Only an emergency indicator light that blinked calmly and at the ready over the door. She shut her eyes on the quiet black and drifted off.

DAY TWO

Tsieh was awakened that morning by McArdle's kiss between his shoulder blades. They had both worked late into the previous night, which wasn't hard with so short a day cycle, and decided they might as well just camp together. After three years, they still called it that. Tsieh was fine with it. McArdle needed their space. Everyone did, on this ship. It was funny how with a mere four people on board (five, now), a whole freighter still felt cramped sometimes. Needing space was natural. Keeping the relationship casual seemed like the best option for everyone.

But what a wonderful way to wake up. The kiss banished the technicolor weirdness his dreams had shown him. It steeled him for the day. Not that he needed steeling—like any day when he got to play with his toys, this had the potential to be a good one.

By the time he got to the kitchen, McArdle had already worked their magic with the coffee, the heavenly aroma permeating every corner of the plastic box they called home. If the smell was going to lose its power some day, it was not today. Instant mood boost.

The mood soured just a little when he saw Lissy's sister sitting alone, a muffin and a cup of coffee on the table between her hands, the brew clearly powerless to affect her. "Hey," he said by way of greeting.

"Yeah? Hi, Tsieh."

"Wrong side of the bed?" he asked, cheerfully. "The first night on a new planet is always the worst." She shifted her gaze to her coffee and said nothing more. He grabbed a muffin from the bin sitting open on the counter and plunked himself down next to McArdle. He'd deal with Therese later. Or he'd let her sister perk her up, if that was even possible.

On cue, Lissy breezed into the kitchen. "Carver's got the trots, so he's out for the day," she announced, helping herself to food and sitting between Tsieh and Therese. "I've put him on web research, to fill out the timeline he made for us."

"Must be his rabbit food," McArdle said between bites. "The nearest satellite's making for spotty connection, so I wouldn't count on Carver contributing all that much."

Lissy didn't disagree, just shrugged. She and McArdle discussed the logistics for their visit to the settlement, while Tsieh watched Therese out of the corner of his eye. She didn't move, except to eat. She was probably listening, but not contributing, which was spooky as hell. Shit, this was gonna be a long day. He answered a few questions about the survey equipment and was about to ask for the status of the camera when Therese looked his way.

"Excuse me, Tsieh, are you ready to leave for the cave?"

Conversation curdled. "I need to finish breakfast and visit the head, but I dunno, twenty minutes?"

Therese nodded. "I'll meet you at the door, I guess." She rinsed her plate and cup and left.

Leave it to McArdle to speak first into the awkwardness. "Yeesh, Boss, how did the same mom make both of you?"

"Don't ask me," Lissy responded. "At least we'll be at the other site today."

"Thanks for nothing," Tsieh said. He regretted it instantly but got only a sympathetic look from Lissy, which made him feel slightly worse. "Is she always so serious?"

"It's what got her the PhD," said Lissy.

Tsieh's appetite deflated. He took one last unenthusiastic bite of his muffin before placing it back in its wrapper. "I better double-check my stuff. Put this in the fridge for me, would you?" McArdle nodded, and Tsieh drained the last of his coffee. Because damned if he wasn't going to drink every drop.

Therese only spoke a few polite words on the walk over to the cave, though she did assist in pushing the dolly full of equipment. By mutual agreement they brought extra air with them and agreed to keep their masks on the whole time, as well as wear gloves. This comity made Tsieh relax a little. He could only hope it was doing the same for her.

The dolly handled surprisingly well through the tunnels, only getting stuck at one tight curve. It cleared the low ceiling, which had been a risk. They kept their lights on the whole time. That, and the simple fact that they'd been here before, should have dulled the drama of stepping into the cavern and seeing the alien flowers on the wall, but it didn't. Not an iota.

Tsieh stood for a moment feeling the purest wonder and joy he had in a long time. It was the sense of discovery, of something not just useful or salable but completely new and unknown. It was rare, and he wanted to savor it. He considered removing his mask and breathing in the unfiltered air, but a glance at the dolly reminded him that it might not be a good idea, even if they had escaped unscathed the last time. He contented himself with the dazzling, infinite colors of the light, and the sense of warmth enveloping him in this dark cave on this barren planet.

"What do you think we should call it?" Therese asked. She stood next to him but her focus was entirely absorbed by the wall. Its beauty reflected in her eyes and on the shiny surface of her mask. "Since we got assigned this job, I think we should get the privilege of naming it, don't you?"

"I've never gotten to name anything," Tsieh answered. It wasn't true. Every piece of tech on that dolly had a name, a personality, but not even McArdle knew them. "Nothing so significant, anyway. Do you have ideas?"

"Oh, tons," Therese said. She sighed. "But maybe we should

do some investigation, make sure we are as accurate as we can be. Where do you want to start?"

Tsieh blinked away from the wall. Therese's face, from what he could tell, was as close to a smile as he'd seen since she joined the crew. "Atmospheric readings first for me," he said. "Double-check for harmful radiation, microbes, toxic gas. You?"

"Pictures," she answered readily, holding up the camera. "And I'll get some accurate measurements. I have paper in my bag, to draw."

"Archaeologists still use paper?"

"If I thought I could, and I had any, I'd tape acetate over the whole wall and trace the images. But . . . negative on both. How about we get started, and we'll see what we find and take it from there. You were able to access the database?"

"Very easy, and nicely organized. Thanks."

She placed the camera on the ground and slid her device out of a pocket. "Fabulous. Here we go."

While Therese took measurement scans, Tsieh squatted next to the dolly. "All right, my pets, time to play," he whispered. Therese didn't seem to notice. "We'll start with you, Xiao. Tell me if anything glows." Xiao was his Geiger-Muller and dosimeter in one, and he adjusted the holo so he could read it from a distance before moving on to Annika for microbial survey. Annika was a rescue, bought secondhand and finicky in her battered casing. She needed finesse, but that he had.

"Hey, Tsieh, can I borrow you for a minute?" Therese called. Giving the instruments a last affectionate tap, he crossed the cavern. "I can't get this camera to work," she said.

"Lemme see." He took the camera and flicked through the last few images taken. Darkness, mostly. Some vague shadows and outlines. Possibly a thumb. "What were you aiming at?"

"The wall," Therese replied, as if it were obvious.

Not from the photos. "I see. That's weird. Hey, look at me?" She complied, and he snapped a photo. They huddled over the viewscreen. "There *you* are. I think. It's like there's no light."

"Is it even possible for something to give off visible light that doesn't show up on a camera?" When Tsieh didn't answer, she added, "I ask because I honestly have no idea. My device is as tech-savvy as I get, which is a bit embarrassing. And its camera is garbage for this, so I wanted to use the stand-alone."

Tsieh aimed square at the wall. The vines and bugs showed up in grainy resolution on the viewscreen, but when he snapped the image, nothing appeared. "Something wrong with the camera, yeah." He navigated through various menus on its control screen, took a few more test shots, shook his head, and handed the camera back to her. She replaced it in her bag with a sigh. "When we get back to the ship, I can fiddle with it more, plug it in and do some experiments. Could be the images just aren't tagging correctly. Could be a driver needs to be installed again."

"I should have brought a backup, but Lissy wanted it for the other site. I'll start drawing." They parted, each to their own corner. Tsieh noted with satisfaction that his equipment was working and chuckled to hide the new fear that it would stop at any moment. He checked the readings. So far, so clear. But it was early.

"So you're an academic, too?" Therese asked from her spot.

She was sitting in front of the wall with a large pad spread on her knees.

Such was his hatred of this topic of conversation, especially with certain participants, that he had specifically instructed Lissy not to tell his sister about his background. He should have known it wouldn't make any difference. "What did your sister tell you?"

"Not much, actually. But yesterday you made a joke about being paid in offprints, and not many people know or use that word."

Xiao was beeping. Tsieh tapped a few selections until it was quiet again and shifted its position slightly. "Fair enough. I'm ABD. It was a while ago."

"What was your subject?" She was sharpening a pencil expertly with a pocketknife.

In for a penny. "Gemology." He waited to see Therese's face go through the usual motions of figuring if the word meant what it sounded like. It wasn't his fault that his field had the dumbest, most obvious name.

But her thoughts were faster, or just plain different, than anyone he'd met at a bar or a party. She was quiet for only half a second before breathing the word "Nerd!" in a tone of teasing but authentic respect. He laughed, and so did she. "How did you get into that?"

"Oh, the usual nerd reasons. I liked science. My parents thought getting a PhD would make me more respectable, if I wasn't going to become a professional. More employable."

"Parents definitely not academics, then."

"Nope. Grad school was cool, for a while. I liked being paid to play with minerals and learn things. I even liked the teaching I had to do for a couple semesters. But I barely started my dissertation."

The last sentence was a dare. Ask me why I didn't finish. Judge me! She didn't take it. Rather she shrugged and said, "It's not for everyone," before returning to the drawing on her lap.

He was a little stung. "It worked for you, though. What was your topic?"

She shrugged again. "Deeply boring. Some of the finer points of archaeological method that, if my royalty checks are any indication, nobody actually cares much about. Sorry." The apology might have been for her snippiness or for her boring dissertation. Tsieh knew better than to press further. He took the pause in conversation to call up the database she'd made and fed it the first data coming from his instruments.

"How did you hook up with my sister? In the business sense, I mean."

"I get it. I met her through McArdle."

"How?"

"You really want to hear this? Isn't it distracting?"

"Not for me if not for you. If I focus too much on drawing I overthink it and it gets weird."

"Okay." Tsieh didn't understand, but as his pets were running themselves now, he had time and he liked the conversation. Therese seemed to be relaxing. "I met McArdle at a bar while I was in grad school. It's cliché but true. They were already a pilot, getting into salvage, and we dated on and off. After a while I couldn't stop thinking about them." Was he getting off topic? Therese didn't seem to mind. "They were working with your sister at the time, just the two of them. They needed more hands. I needed an adventure. And no one says no to McArdle."

"Really?" Therese paused and looked over at him.

"Not like that." He blushed. "I mean, McArdle has this way about them. They know who they are, what they want, and they do what they need to get it. I was struggling with my topic and being grounded and it just looked like the two of them were on an exciting voyage every week. When I realized I could still use what I'd learned, but also fly around to different planets? I was sold."

"I wish I were so adventurous." She sounded like she meant it.

"Well, you're here, right?"

Therese paused. "I didn't really have a choice."

He wanted to press for a deeper answer, but the readouts caught his attention. "Hey," he said, "There's something weird here. Can you check it out?"

Therese placed her paper on the ground, carefully laid the pencil on it, and walked over to look at his monitor with him. To her credit, she didn't pretend she knew what she was reading. "I don't know what I'm reading," she said. "Everything looks stable. Is there something dangerous?"

"Nothing. The radiation levels are where I thought they would be, no worries. But look at Annika . . . I mean, the green line here. That machine is looking for microbes in the air."

"It's not showing anything, is it? And my laptop in grad school was Cornelius."

Cool. "Exactly. Almost nothing. As if there's nothing alive in this cavern. Which is weird."

"Is it working all right?"

Tsieh lifted his mask and breathed on the sensor. The needle jumped, the readout made a little hill, and a list climbed up the side of the display. He replaced his mask. "Seems fine. But this isn't a lifeless planet. You have the birds outside, for one thing."

"The ones with the leathery wings? They were eating something yesterday, so whatever that was lives here too." Therese paled. Or perhaps it was just the shifting glow from the wall.

"You find life like that, it follows that even smaller, invisible life is around too. But my instruments aren't picking up anything. In the air, anyway. I should probably scrape the rocks on the ground."

"No, I don't think so." Her tone was like Lissy's bossy tone, but with a colder edge to it. Damn. So much for warming up. "I mean, yes, obviously. You're right. But I also think we should take a sample of the wall."

"Really?" He looked around, as if Lissy would burst in and surprise them at any minute. "I don't want to damage the find."

"Believe me, neither do I, but I'd really feel a lot more comfortable going forward if we knew what the hell we were looking at. If we collect from one of the corners, I don't think that'll be a problem." Her voice turned dreamy, like she was talking to herself.

"You're the archaeologist. Let me get some sample containers together. Are you okay?"

"What?" She shook herself, visibly. "Sorry. I didn't get much sleep last night. And I had dreams . . . "

"God, me too."

"It's just so exciting. I always have trouble sleeping when I'm excited." It felt like half-truth, but Tsieh let it go. Emotions sometimes ran weird on a job. "So go ahead, take some samples," she said. "Tell me how I can help. And then, let's settle on a provisional name for this. Not having one is starting to creep me out."

He grabbed a glass vial and a tweezer from the dolly. Together he and she knelt by the lower corner, where a vine escaped ground that wasn't there, turning from purple to sickly green as it traveled the wall. He scraped gently, delicately, as if he expected the vine to whip around and attack him or scream at the pain. Neither happened. The tip of the tweezer scraped solid rock. He pressed harder, until something broke off and landed in the vial, which sealed itself automatically. He held it up to examine more closely. None of the light had been captured.

"More weirdness, Tsieh?"

He shook his head. "I'll feed this to what I have here, but . . . I expected a perceptible layer on the rocks. It's like it's not even there."

"Are we hallucinating this? All of us, the same thing?"

She was serious. Ridiculous though it sounded out loud, Tsieh found himself sharing her worry. "Let's test it. What do you see?"

Therese briefly shut her eyes before looking again at the wall. "An explosion of beauty and life, captured in two dimensions like stained glass. It glows. There are vines and flowers and insects. This vine is greenish-blue, and it terminates in a flower, or maybe a set of branches, like spider legs spun from steel." She traced it with a finger.

"We're seeing the same thing." Tsieh nodded. "There's nothing in the air, and we're both masked."

"We took them off yesterday." Therese's eyes widened above her mask, which fogged visibly with her increased breath. She was more than serious. She was on the edge of panicking.

Tsieh moved closer and put a hand on her shoulder, gently drawing her into eye contact as she sank back onto her butt. "Hey, look at me. The air is safe. I checked it, and your sister checked it—she wouldn't put us in danger. It's okay." He saw the calm return, decided to risk a joke. "If you freak out, you won't be able to complete this expedition. Think of the offprints!" She laughed at that, a real laugh that lit her eyes. He smiled back, but it wasn't as pure. If all PhDs were this high-strung, he had definitely dodged a bullet. He'd have to thank McArdle when he got home.

"You know that you're sharing the byline," she said, and his smile left him. "I'm serious. We couldn't do this properly without you. I'll even split the offprints."

And the smile was back. He stood slowly, helping her to her feet. "One thing at a time. We were going to name this?"

Therese was again facing the wall, its flora and fauna. The color washed out her face, reminding Tsieh of old CRTs on static, or blue screens of death from beloved ancient computers. But her face was alive in a way the ghoulish color could not explain or remove. "It looks like it should be hard, as if it's glass. Even as it glows, and the glow is warm. It should be cold, and slick." She raised a hand, and Tsieh noticed too late that she had removed her glove. Probably to help her hold the pencil for sketching. Her hand hovered over the glowing surface of the wall. Tsieh seized her wrist to pull it away.

"Probably don't want to touch it like that," he said. She didn't fight his grip as he lowered her hand. She looked at him with calm curiosity. It made his insides cold, despite the warmth of the cave.

Her face fell for the space of a second, collapsed as if on the verge of tears. But none came. Instead she resumed her businesslike expression. He released her hand and she searched the ground until she found her glove and replaced it. It did less to soothe him than he thought it should. "Nothing about this is making any sense, Tsieh."

"No disagreement there."

"Can I be honest with you, and you won't tell Lissy?"

He nodded.

"I am completely over my head here. I don't know what this is. I have serious doubts that humans made it, because I can't even tell what it's made of. Can you?"

He shrugged. "I may, later, but right now, I'm with you. This doesn't make sense." He shook the vial in his hand and heard the small chips of rock rattle against the glass. "If I tell Lissy anything, it'll only be that we're both stumped."

"If we tell her that, she'll probably want to bring someone else in to look at it."

"No, she won't." He spoke the words with a heavy finality, hoping she'd pick it up. Therese looked around, as if she were afraid someone else was listening. Tsieh understood the feeling.

"Can I ask you something?" Therese asked, voice low. "What exactly happened on your last job? Lissy keeps dancing around it and I don't want to push her."

Of course, Lissy wouldn't tell her sister about that. "It went bad. We hooked up with another outfit, one we thought was reputable, to take on a huge operation. Another colony, bigger and messier than this one. By the time we showed up, they'd already cleaned out everything of value. They did a shitty job, too, left the place . . . well, the phrase *toxic dump* comes to mind. We got the blame for it. Haven't been able to shift it since." Tsieh cringed just thinking about it, and he hadn't been the one who set it up. "That's the last time Lissy trusted anyone outside of us."

"Yeah, I know trust is a problem for her," Therese said bitterly.

"I'm sure she trusts you, or she wouldn't have brought you in. This whole thing is a leap of faith. For all of us."

Therese looked to her wrist for the watch that wasn't there. "How much longer do we have to work?"

Tsieh pulled out his device and tapped it. "Sun goes down in about four hours. Lissy wants us all home by then. Don't know what monsters might be waiting in the dark."

She cleared her throat and resumed her position before the wall, taking up again her pad and pencil. "Guess we'd better get back to work." She smiled, weakly. "Thanks, Tsieh. For telling me, and for everything you're doing."

"No problem." He went back to the dolly to check the readouts and make sure everything was copying into the database, which he'd downloaded to local physical drives for convenience. He'd beam it to the ship servers in stages. He paused in the middle of naming a file and called over to Therese. "Hey? How about we just call it 'the anomaly'? At least, for now."

Therese stopped sketching but didn't look up. "I think it's perfect," she said.

McArdle shut their eyes against the delicious lurch of the jumpship taking off, opening them as they effortlessly brought it to a cruising altitude. They were able to get Lissy into the air in time to see Therese and Tsieh pushing the dolly to the cave. They hoped that the archaeologist knew how to handle her share of its weight. There was no need to warn the professor to take care of Tsieh, even if the reverse were a requirement. Tsieh had a good head on his shoulders and could take care of himself.

Lissy was staring out the window as the drab scenery flew by, tapping her feet against the floor so hard they sounded over the normal vibrations of the ship. "You okay, Boss?" McArdle called over to her.

"Just excited. Aren't you?"

McArdle loved Lissy, they did, but she was not cute when she was insecure. "I'll be thrilled when we land and see what there is to sell. You got the map Tsieh and I made?"

"Yeah." Lissy called up the map on her device, matching the image currently displayed on the ship's main screen. Lines of light overlaid the view of the ground. "This looks pretty standard to me."

"You wanna start with the mining or the living section?"

"Your call. We just have to remember to write down everything, not just what we're taking. Therese was insistent."

"Yeah, I heard." McArdle did not take orders, or even suggestions, from most people. The exception was family, which included both the people loving and supporting them from another planet and the crew of the *Maris Stella*. They thought about how their beloved egghead would play this. They remembered Tsieh's smile and figured his positive attitude would carry everyone through. Again. "I suggest we start with the mining office. It might give us some clues about where the op was when they abandoned. We can tour the living facilities afterwards, then the mines themselves."

"Right, as usual."

They crested the ridge behind the cave and it took McArdle only a little longer to find the mines, hone in on the central mining office, and find a place to set the ship down. They and Lissy stepped out of the ship wearing protective gear, because you never knew what these old mines belched out, even after years had passed. Mostly it was dust. Clearly the electric shields holding it in had failed. Brown powder coated their masks and jackets and led both to put on goggles, which they wiped every so often with their gloves and cursed. "Typical shithole," said McArdle, to Lissy's nod.

They followed the outlines of a road or path which led them to a collection of the usual prefab buildings, looking like toy blocks under sawdust. McArdle noted some vehicles and stepped closer to brush the detritus from one. Peering through the glass, they guessed it might be functional, or could be made so again. That would be useful, if they stayed longer on this rock. They made a note to find fuel and were about to tell Lissy the idea, but the boss had disappeared.

McArdle followed the footprints in the sand, which led into

the largest of the square buildings. They pushed through the outer doors and shook off as much dust as they could before entering the office through the inner doors and removing their goggles. The room was warehouse-dark, and they turned on their flashlight.

It reminded McArdle of fire drills at school. After lining up outside, you'd return to the room, and it would be just as you left it. You picked up your pencil and went back to work, but minutes were missing and they haunted you for the rest of the day. How much time haunted this place?

Lissy was already walking among the desks, cubicles, and chairs that waited in ordered ranks for their people to return, her own light caressing what remained. Every so often she stopped, fussed through the contents of a desk, and moved on. McArdle decided to follow her example. The desk nearest them was neat, all the supplies in their place. The owner had affixed small plush animals to the cubicle wall with tacks, a mosaic of fuzz simultaneously charming and disturbing, beady plastic eyes staring from lolling heads, pierced limbs sporting expanding holes. Leaning their flashlight a little closer, McArdle could see the computer in the middle of the desk remained plugged into the strip behind it. The screen was clear of dust and they tapped it once or twice before feeling around the casing for buttons. No reaction. No power. Whatever juice fed the machines was long gone. The batteries had probably rotted, rendering the tech useless. They picked up the computer and turned it over, hoping to be wrong. They weren't. The next desk yielded the same results. "Boss!" they called.

"What is it, McArdle?" Lissy had disappeared into the dark.

McArdle could see her light past the edge of a door. Break room? That would track. Lissy emerged, the mask and distance making her expression unreadable. “Find something?”

“All the computers are here,” McArdle said, replacing the unit in their hand and sweeping the flashlight over the desks, nearly all of which had a black rectangle in the middle. “Why not take these when they evacuated? In fact . . . ” They walked around the perimeter of the room, inspecting the walls of cubicles. Some were plainer than others, but each had at least a photo, a company calendar, a pennant for a sports team, proudly displayed. “Why didn’t they take any of the personal stuff?”

“Emergency?” Lissy’s words dovetailed nicely with McArdle’s visions of a fire drill. “Like a chemical spill or gas leak?”

“And they never came back?” Even with the power out and long-dead cleaning bots neglecting the floors and windows, the office seemed almost ready for business. “Where did they go?”

“Home.”

“But the cars are still outside.”

“Not many. This kind of complex often has a shuttle between living and working quarters.” Lissy coughed. “And there’s always the possibility that they were home from work when shit went down, so they never had to evacuate the office in the first place. Let’s take some pictures and do a tech scan. You ready?”

“Of course.” McArdle reached into a deep pocket and produced their device, which they left on a central table. The machine beeped before emitting a thin red laser that scanned the room from ceiling to floor. It would not only take measurements but register the ID chips of any useful tech and organize it into a list. How's that for a database, Professor? they thought with the tiniest smirk.

Lissy took her camera, the twin to the one Tsieh had left with that morning, and snapped a few dozen shots from different positions. They moved as a team into the break room, even the restrooms, documenting everything.

"That should be enough data to pore through tonight," Lissy said, heading back to the door. "They certainly left plenty of goodies here. Let's go see what the residences were like."

The residential area was equally unsettling. More prefab buildings, once surrounded by an energy fence to keep the dust and wild creatures at bay, but it was drained of power. The houses sat like dark, squat mushrooms in the dust. McArdle and Lissy entered a few easily, since their electric locks were nonfunctional. The interiors were neat and spare. The central halls, where workers would have been served meals and entertainment, waited for the next use with chairs on tables and everything pushed against the wall. The kitchens were still stocked.

Like the offices, the barracks bore all the signs of living but nothing alive. Beds were neatly made, or the sheets left dented by absent bodies. Personal effects were taped to walls, stashed under mattresses, scattered on small tables.

"Why is all their shit here?" McArdle asked.

"They evacuated," Lissy said, sweeping her light over the plastic floor of the hallway, counting the rooms of the unit they were in. She spoke quickly, soothingly. McArdle had the distinct impression they were being shushed, and did not care for it.

"Evacuate the offices, evacuate the living quarters—you know what that looks like, right?" McArdle went into one of the rooms and began to paw through the cheap chests of drawers lining one wall. Five or more people would have shared the space, and it was all here. Clothing. Toothbrushes. Religious accessories. If they dug deeper, they suspected they would find more intimate personal belongings. "They didn't take any of their stuff, and they didn't make a mess. It's always a mess, when you have to evacuate." McArdle didn't like the memories flashing through their mind and spoke louder to chase them away. "Boss, what actually happened to these people? There have to be records."

"I assumed they just abandoned the colony."

"You assumed?" McArdle slammed the drawer closed. The piece of garbage made only the quietest thud, catching on cloth within.

"I put everything we got on my sister's database," Lissy said. "We have all the petty, standard complaints from the colonists about food and money, and then we have nothing. They left."

"What if they didn't? Back at the office complex, you said gas leak."

"It wasn't a toxic leak. I don't think so. They would have mentioned that in reports to the company."

"Unless no one was around to make a report."

"There aren't any bodies."

McArdle shivered. The crew had dealt with bodies on plenty of previous jobs. Bodies would have been preferable. Bodies made sense and came with a protocol. They called up their map, now dotted with more accurate measurements and inventory. In the northern corner, beyond the barracks, the data grew fuzzy. "Remember this?" they said to their boss. "These areas here. Tsieh and I thought they were natural, but we weren't sure. Could they be more caves, where people sheltered? Hell, maybe someone's still there."

Lissy sucked in a breath. The sound through the mask would have been almost comical, if both of them didn't know how survivors ruined salvage claims. "We'll do a flyby after we check out the mines. I guess for now we just document everything." She held out the camera and paused before taking a shot. "Though I don't know if we really have to, beyond our scan. I mean, it's not related to the art in the wall."

The waffling was out of character and annoying. "Maybe you should call your sister and ask her what she wants us to do."

The words were sharper than they intended, and Lissy winced. "I don't need to check in with her."

"On a normal salvage, absolutely. You're the one trying to make this into something else, so it's your call. Boss."

"Fine." Lissy took out her device and tapped at it angrily, shook it, and tapped it again. McArdle held their hand out automatically. Lissy handed it over and spat, "No connection."

"Should be. We have a pretty clear path to the ship." McArdle flipped the device around, tried to send the message again, got nothing. The wifi came from the ship, routed through the jump, but nothing was getting through. They handed it back to Lissy only to have the same lack of luck with their own. "It's possible that all the dust outside is messing with the signals, or something is still running and putting out a competing frequency."

Lissy put her device away. "I'm sure it's just a glitch."

"All right, I'm just gonna say it. Something is weird about this place. That cave, the site, none of it makes sense, and we're splashing around in it half-assed."

Lissy's eyes flashed. McArdle fought with her on plenty of missions, so the look was comforting and invigorating at the same time. They prepared for a verbal throw down, but then the boss said, "Yeah, I agree. It's weird. But we'll figure it out. For now, let's take some pictures and head to the jump. We've got the flyby you mentioned to do before it gets dark, and we don't know what other surprises are waiting for us."

"Never do," said McArdle as Lissy snapped a picture of the room.

The mines themselves provided mostly positive surprises. The tiny offices and cubicles peppered around the operation proper had the look of a perpetual weekend: desk neat, ready for work on Monday. The machinery was all pretty new and in good shape and shielded from the dust. McArdle got one drill spinning again, so it was safe to say that it all worked or, at the very least, contained healthy parts that would sell on their own. Transport would be a bitch, but nothing they hadn't seen before. Lissy, who had been silent and distracted since they left the barracks, perked up. Together she and McArdle estimated the potential yield and found it very good.

The sun was just starting to sink as they got in the jump for their last stop. It wasn't supposed to be a stop, but a salvor's life is full of surprises. McArdle took the jump past the mine entrance and out into the desert, where the mysterious mounds were outlined on the map. "See them below?" McArdle asked.

"I do." Lissy had her face pressed to the window. "Can't make them out from this height. You think it's another cave system? Maybe we'll find more art. Or survivors."

McArdle brought the ship lower, skimming as close as they dared to the mounds. They passed, turned, and passed again, banking to give the two of them the best view of the ground. The force of the engine passing blew some of the dry sand from the mounds into flattened puffs, parted like hair. The shapes below became clearer. More symmetrical.

"Those aren't caves, Boss," said McArdle. They didn't add any more information, tuning out Lissy's repeated questions while setting the ship down into the soft surface before the mounds. It was proper desert out here, the sand deep and golden, not like the earwax-colored crap covering the offices and dorms. They reset their face mask and goggles and stepped out of the ship, Lissy behind them. Wind pulled the sand this way and that, covering, revealing. With a gloved hand they scooped at a shallow depression, revealing metal printed with words and numbers.

"I think we just found the colonists' ships," they said.

Therese and Tsieh's last few hours in the cave had been

productive. Therese had completed a general overview drawing of the anomaly, a map of its imagery more than anything else, as well as a few detailed sketches of specific flowers or insects. It was the most soothing time she'd ever spent on an expedition: letting the colored light play over her, losing herself in the twisting, blooming splendor. She relaxed, eyes half-closed, breathing in and out so gently there was hardly any mist on her mask. Whenever she shook herself out of the trance, a new drawing was there on her lap, though she did not remember plotting the lines.

Now she spread the drawings out over the table back in the galley while Tsieh was in the lab, putting the samples he'd collected through machines whose names, affectionate or official, she couldn't keep track of. She found she missed him. He was the first person on this expedition who actually seemed to understand what it was she did for a living. She'd long since given up explaining it to Lissy. Their mother had never understood either, though she praised the life choice with all the pride of a parent watching her beloved child enter the priesthood or the Peace Corps, or swear a presidential oath. Therese's career was appropriate, it was distinguished, it was the mark of someone who had realized her potential. But working with Tsieh, she felt something she hadn't in years: fun. She enjoyed telling him about her methods and learning from his point of view. He was so damned smart, but easy to talk to. It was a shame they were only going to be colleagues for this one project. Though maybe . . .

"Hey." It was McArdle striding into the kitchen. Therese blushed as if caught, though for what, she wasn't sure. It didn't matter. McArdle barely looked at her, scanning the room instead. Their clothing, utilitarian though it was, was smeared with dust. More worrisome was the look in their eyes: distant and skittery.

Therese looked at her device. "You guys are kinda late getting back. Did you find anything?"

"I dunno. Maybe. Where's Tsieh?" McArdle bit off each word with impatience.

"Lab," said Therese. "What happened?"

McArdle didn't even pretend to listen and was gone before Therese finished her question. She replayed the conversation in her mind. The pilot and she hadn't gotten off to a good start, maybe, but tonight they seemed really tense. Most likely, Therese reasoned, something had happened with Lissy. It would make perfect sense. She couldn't be the only one butting heads with her sister.

Like the Devil at the sound of his name, Lissy strode into the galley. She had shucked her overalls and her regular clothing was clean, her feet bare. Her face was flushed. Overall it was a healthy, relaxed mien totally at odds with McArdle's. Therese was not looking forward to handling it.

Lissy greeted her sister and stood beside her, taking in the drawings on the table, occasionally pulling one by its corners to get a better view. Therese put her hands in her lap to hide their nervous fluttering. Lissy's gaze lit on a page that showed a particularly gnarly collection of vines. Therese was rather proud of the details on that one. Lissy lifted it gently from the table and held it out at arm's length, staring in silence for some moments. Finally, she spoke. "This is good, T."

"They're just sketches," Therese said, but her voice cracked a little. She swallowed. "We couldn't get the camera to work. Did yours do better? Because I think I want to try again tomorrow. We really should have photos."

"I mean, this is really good. You post some of your drawings on your feeds, but in person, it's really something."

That Lissy saw her feeds was not news. That she noticed? That was something else. "I'm glad you like it."

Lissy put the paper back on the table with near-reverence. "When people see this, it's gonna change everything. We, you and me, are gonna change everything."

"Okay." Therese wasn't sure what other response was appropriate. She tilted her head towards the door, wondering if McArdle had found Tsieh and when they were coming back. It was past suppertime, and Therese was getting a little hungry. A lot hungry.

"How's Carver doing?" Lissy asked.

Oh, shit. Therese's stomach dropped. She'd forgotten about Carver completely. "I don't know."

"You mean you didn't check on him?" Lissy said, her voice weirdly intense.

"I didn't know I was supposed to." She scrabbled for the pride she'd felt a moment ago, before it curled and burned into schoolyard shame. "I'm sure he's fine."

"But you don't know?" Lissy took a deep breath through her nostrils, a quiet roar in reverse. Her voice remained quiet but dropped an octave. "Look, I know you don't like him . . . "

"I never said that!"

"And I know that you have a hard time with people, but we're a team here. That includes you, now, so I need you start looking out for us. We're all in this together."

Therese closed her eyes and wished to disappear. Why did it always go this way, whenever she and Lissy seemed like they were connecting? And why did it always seem to be Therese's fault?

"Look, I'm sorry. I can check on him now, all right?" She started to rise, but Lissy put a hand on her shoulder. It was surprisingly warm.

"Don't bother. I'm the one responsible, here." Then she was gone—like McArdle, leaving no room for a reply. Therese was alone with her drawings, wondering if she'd ever get being a part of a group right.

Tsieh had finished setting up some tests to run and was about to head to the galley for dinner and reports when McArdle came into the lab. He took one look at them and drew them into a hug. They hugged back, but it was tense. He pulled away. "Was it that bad? Was it like Cottonwood?"

McArdle laughed, but it was distant and hollow. "Nothing could be as bad as Cottonwood. I couldn't get the smell out of my clothes for weeks. Sometimes I still smell it. How did bodies even get . . . ?" They stopped, bit their lips.

Tsieh moved his hands to take theirs. "Was it like . . . before the Mercy Center?" He was tiptoeing around the part of their life he knew only from what they'd told him—which was plenty but somehow never enough.

McArdle pulled away. "Just say InDevCo, all right, Tsieh? I told you. And it wasn't like InDevCo's evacuation, either. I don't even know that there was an evac. It's just . . . empty over there."

"Empty?"

Before he could press further, there was a knock. Lissy stuck her head in and asked, "Either of you seen Carver?"

"Not lately," said Tsieh. "What did he do?"

"I can't find him." Lissy stepped full into the lab. McArdle turned away from Tsieh to face her, maybe grateful that their conversation was over. "He's not in his room, not in the cargo bay. Not here. Where the fuck did he go?"

Tsieh truly had no idea, but he was a tad annoyed at the interruption. "He could have gone to stretch his legs, maybe, and you missed him?"

"Sometimes you need fresh air after a bout of the runs," said McArdle, nonchalant. They headed out of the lab. "I'm gonna go put a pot on. Tsieh, help me?"

Tsieh fell into step beside them, but Lissy kept pace behind. "This planet doesn't really have fresh air, McArdle. And it's getting dark. He knows better than to go out alone at night."

"Does he?" McArdle walked faster.

Therese heard the voices coming down the hall. McArdle came in first and went directly to the coffee press, where they measured out grounds. The scent hit fast, and Therese's muscles relaxed at it. Tsieh sank into a chair, smiling at her and shifting the papers into a neater pile to clear himself a bit of space. Then he planted his elbows on the table and rested his head in his hands. His tiredness echoed hers.

"Carver's an alleycat, Boss. He doesn't stay in just because you need him to."

Therese waited for Lissy to turn on McArdle, to cut them with words or at least get defensive and huffy. But Lissy just shook her head. "All the other cats are here."

The coffee press bubbled.

"Am I to understand," Therese ventured, "that Carver isn't in his room? Is he okay? Where did he go?"

"Hang on," said Tsieh, tapping his screen. "I'm trying to track his device, but if he doesn't . . . " Tsieh frowned and rubbed a hand through his hair. "I can't get a connection here, either. Shit. Something is weird with the comms, on top of everything."

"You guys, too?" McArdle asked, leaving the coffee to look at Tsieh's device over his shoulder. "We couldn't reach you two when we were out at the colony. I thought it was something wrong on the jump, but you can't get connected here, either? Shit."

"Guys, we gotta find him." Lissy was quiet, deflated.

Therese felt the stab of guilt again. Beyond that was something that had been nagging at her since Lissy's first speech to the crew, since the pictures in the cave. She said in her most reasonable voice, "If Carver left the ship, there are only so many places he could go, and not a lot of room to get lost in between. He could have gone towards the colony."

McArdle shook their head. "It's a long walk, and there's that ridge. I don't see him making the climb."

Therese waited for the interruption to run its course.

"Exactly. So he's probably headed for the cave. But I'm worried that if he's sick, he might get confused, and there were all those tunnels we haven't mapped yet."

Lissy let out a little noise.

"I'm sure he's okay," Therese said quickly, to soothe her sister and prepare her for what came next. "If I'm right, we better move and get him back here for the night. If Lissy thinks that's a good idea." Lissy nodded, first to Therese, then the others, who all seemed to agree. Good. Now for the stinger. "After that, we need to get off this planet."

"What?" cried Lissy.

"At least temporarily. We need to get Carver some medical attention, and we need to bring more people in to help us."

"No." The word was a door slamming shut. "That's not how this is going to work."

"Would you trust me for once in your life?" Therese rose to meet her sister eye to eye, anger to anger. "I can't work that cave by myself. I'm just an archaeologist. You need a geologist, a planetary expert, a radiologist, whatever -ologists handle something this weird. Tsieh is doing amazing work, but we need more hands and eyes."

"I said no, T," said Lissy. "We can't leave."

"She's right, Boss." McArdle poured the first cup of coffee and handed it to Tsieh, who perked up a little as he breathed in the aroma. They poured themself a cup too and sat down beside him. "Lissy and I found something weird, too. The entire mining colony is deserted, but deserted like they woke up, had breakfast, and left. Nothing was packed. Nothing was taken. There's no mess. It's just empty, waiting for them to come back."

Tsieh took McArdle's hand. Lissy looked like she was going to add something, but Therese ignored her. "Do we expect them to come back?"

McArdle shook their head. "We found their ships. Looked like the full complement for a colony that size. They need some repairs, but they can fly. They're also perfectly neat, clean except for the sand, and *empty*." They looked into Tsieh's eyes. He set his lips and squeezed their hand tighter. "I don't know where the people went. I don't know how they left."

"Maybe they sent out a distress signal and someone picked them up," Lissy said, but her ragged tone showed even she didn't believe it.

"Not with working ships, they didn't," said Tsieh. He looked at Therese's pictures and flipped the top one over to a blank side. "McArdle's right. This is too weird."

Therese went to the cabinet and removed two more mugs and filled them with coffee. She placed one in front of Lissy, who had surrendered and now sat in the last chair. Therese remained standing to sip hers, putting a hand on her sister's shoulder. "We can deal with that later. The priority now is Carver. We have to go find him. Maybe McArdle and I can go?"

"I have to come, too," said Lissy. She hadn't touched her cup.

"Of course." And maybe, Therese thought, maybe I can get another look at the anomaly and correct some gaps in my sketches. "But after we find him, we get out of here. Or I won't help with anything else."

Lissy looked too tired to argue, settled for being petty. "Doesn't go your way, you quit, I guess?"

"Me, too," said McArdle. "Boss, I want this to work as much

as you do. But we need to step back and regroup. I don't think we have a choice." Lissy's mouth opened to respond. "I'm serious. I fly this boat, and there's only one direction I'm going once everyone's back on board. Even if you don't come with."

"We may have another problem." Tsieh drained his cup. "If Carver is sick, how do we know it's just food poisoning? I don't want the rest of us to get it."

"We haven't yet," said Lissy. But her color was high and there was a sheen to her skin. Was it just the stress?

"We need to quarantine him," Tsieh said.

Lissy sighed. "Fine. Lock him in his room."

"No." Tsieh stood up. "If it's airborne, if he picked something up on this planet when you guys were scouting, we need to seal him off. And there's only one way to do that. We disable the jump and put him inside. At least until we can figure out what's wrong and get him help. If it's just stomach upset, he'll be bored but fine. If it's not?" Tsieh waved his hands in the air. "I don't know. We may all be exposed anyway. But it's the best I can think of. I'm not a doctor."

"We don't have any useful doctors in this crew. You're the closest, so we'll listen to you." Lissy nodded to McArdle. "Find my sister a complete hazmat suit. Hell, if Carver left his behind, maybe that'll fit. Let's gear up and get out, full masks and air, and bring our man home."

Carver had not, in fact, left his suit behind. This was reassuring from a safety perspective but left Therese to wear the crew's backup suit, which was a size too large and smelled of storage. Therese shifted her weight and the durable white plastic crackled. Her mask creaked against her goggles. She hated having all these layers between her and the world. At least Lissy looked almost as ridiculous in her getup, even if it fit her better. Only McArdle seemed totally at ease, approaching the ship exit pushing Tsieh's dolly, now empty of equipment but for a single first-aid kit.

"Figured since we don't know what condition he's in, this might be useful. Tsieh tells me the dolly'll fit through the tunnels," they said.

Therese confirmed this, and envied McArdle their serenity and flexibility.

Together the three clomped down the ramp and onto the ground outside the ship. Lissy fired up her lantern, a powerful industrial model that created an orb of yellow light around them, and set it up on the dolly. The darkness beyond its light was so sharp Therese was sure she could touch it, like the skin of a bubble. Beyond that skin the sun was down, and smaller lights replaced it. This sky sported no moon, but the stars were countless and reassuring. She'd grown up, done her research, and gotten her degree in cities. It was only when she was on expeditions that she was far enough from light pollution to see stars. Back in Saqqara, the lights so thickly blanketed the sky that she'd wondered how the ancients ever picked which to follow. Intelligent life hadn't spent long enough on this planet to assign stories to its constellations, so the sky was a fresh set of paints. You could play and create whatever images you wanted to. If only you had time. If a member of your team weren't missing. If McArdle wasn't waving a hand in your face to get your attention.

"Tracks," said McArdle. The others shuffled to clear a path for the light. Indeed, there were boot prints leading away from the ship in the only direction that they could go: the cave. Therese was back on familiar ground. Follow the evidence of human involvement. This was just another dig. She was in control.

"How did you miss him on your way back?" Lissy asked. "He must have walked right past you."

"No," Therese said, refusing the implied blame. "Look closer. See how the set going out are so much sharper? Tsieh and I walked through here, what, an hour and a half ago? Carver walked out much more recently."

"Well, maybe if you'd checked in with him when you got home, he wouldn't have been able to sneak out."

"All right, you two." McArdle pushed the dolly and themself between the quarreling sisters and walked forward, keeping their feet to the side of the tracks. "Let's march. We don't have all night and we don't know what beasties are out there."

Therese took the point. Lights shone not only in the sky but in scattered pairs and groups amid the surface darkness, reflecting beams from the lantern. Blinking. Moving. Could be something as harmless as the creature she found yesterday. Or could be more like what ate it. She and Lissy fell into line with McArdle. Their suits crinkled and clicked; the lantern hummed. The sounds distracted Therese from thoughts of McArdle's beasties. Of course, they might also make it harder to hear anything approach until it was too late. Therese shivered and focused on staying close to the protective yellow light.

The tracks continued, clear and deep, as if Carver were trying to make himself findable. Nothing intersected them and there was no sign of creatures approaching or interfering. As they arrived at the cave, Lissy said, "Damn," and stooped to pick something up. "He took off his mask."

"Gloves, too," said McArdle, holding one of them.

Therese's own gloves were stiff, rubbery, and making her sweat even in the cold alien night. She wanted to grab the fingers in her teeth and rip them off, but the mask blocked her. Maybe Carver had had the same thought.

The cave was different at night. The face of the mountain reflected the lantern, its rock like matte gold. The cave mouth, however, loomed like a hole torn in space.

"There's a chance he got lost in one of the tunnels," said Lissy, "but I think that's unlikely. In any case, we should stick together. First we'll check the main cavern where the thing is."

"The anomaly." McArdle and Lissy turned to look at Therese. "Tsieh and I decided to call it that, if it works for you, until we learn better what it is." Lissy looked away.

McArdle shrugged. "Lissy, you're right. We go to the main cavern first. Carver's probably there. Lead the way."

McArdle had only walked this path once, Therese twice, but they followed with assurance, the dolly filling the tunnel and keeping Lissy in the lead. Other branches beckoned, but they ignored them. How familiar it felt. In the myth, Daedalus met his king's challenge to thread a conch shell by tying string to an ant and baiting the shell with honey. Therese thought she could find her way to the main cavern much easier than an ant tracking honey—even blindfolded, guided by some sense that humans hadn't yet accurately described. The anomaly was compelling, and not just professionally. She wished she'd brought her sketchbook, even if it was kind of inappropriate to the situation.

The blackness of the walls and the tightening of the space tamed the brightness of the lantern. Therese kept her eyes down, waiting for the blue glow to start, indicating they were close.

"Carver!" Lissy called. The name echoed off the walls but got no response.

McArdle gave it a shot. "Are you hiding in here, you weasel? Not funny."

"There's no spoor in here." Therese only became aware she'd spoken out loud when McArdle gave her a look. "Sorry. You said *weasel.* It made me think. Where are the animals? You'd think this cave would be a shelter at night, with whatever predators might be out there. But I've never seen a single dropping in here, have you?"

"Jesus, T, focus, would you? Carver!" Lissy's shout rang against the walls, but too briefly.

McArdle sidled closer to Therese and spoke in a low voice. "If there are creatures in here, I bet all this noise is pissing them off." Then, louder: "Boss, cool it. We're almost there, and the shouting is making everything confusing."

"Right. Shit."

After the plosive of Lissy's response faded in the air, McArdle said, again to Therese, "I swear, she couldn't do anything without me."

Therese grinned, grateful her mask covered it. The party

smoothly passed the dip of the tunnel ceiling. She said, "Lissy, we're here. Kill the light."

"Like hell I will."

Therese was annoyed that she would be robbed of the drama of seeing the anomaly in its glory upon entering the cave. It was also blasphemy to Therese's conservationist instincts. The yellow glow washed out the colors, turning all the depicted plant life a sickly, dying green. Could it be harmed by bright light? There was no time to ask. Kneeling before the wall, bare hands outstretched, was Carver. He still wore his suit, but his head was completely uncovered. His hair stood away like he'd gotten a fright and no chance to smooth it down afterwards. Every so often his hands twitched, like a dog dreaming.

His hands were also, upon closer inspection, sinking into the surface of the anomaly by a few centimeters. Therese could still see his fingers, but the stems and petals of flowers seemed to float over them. She gasped.

McArdle and Lissy hurried to their crewmate's side, calling his name as they strapped on his mask. The lantern they left behind at the cave entrance, blocking the darkness from coming any closer but throwing sharp, jangly shadows against the cave walls that made Therese a little nauseated. Lissy pressed her fingers to Carver's neck. "I've got a pulse. He's also really warm, maybe a fever? Fuck, I wish we had a real doctor in this crew sometimes."

"What do we do about his hands?" McArdle asked. Lissy looked at the obscured fingers, as if seeing them for the first time. She drew in a breath, reaching up with her own hand to touch Carver's exposed wrist. "Can we pull him out?" McArdle asked.

Therese, still queasy, answered them. "We have to try. But do it slowly. Carefully."

Lissy took one of his arms and McArdle the other, with Therese putting a useless hand on his shoulder. McArdle counted to three and the two of them pulled, slow and steady. There was no resistance. His hands came clear, though he held them out even after they were freed. Therese snatched the first aid kit from the dolly and cracked the plastic case open. McArdle swiftly took out a roll of gauze and wiped off Carver's hands. The gauze remained dry and bore no discoloration.

Carver said nothing while they ministered to him. Therese wasn't sure he even blinked. McArdle put their hands under his armpits and attempted to lift him but met no success. Lissy called his name over and over again, pulling at his arm, her voice growing higher and more desperate each time. Finally she stopped and simply hung on him. "Wake up," she begged in a hoarse whisper.

"I'll get the dolly closer and we'll put him on," said McArdle.

Therese approached cautiously. She examined Carver's hands, his long, delicate fingers. The veins stood out between the bones and she touched them gingerly. They felt like wires buried in plastic. She noted with surprise that his fingernails were painted with a shimmery mother-of-pearl sheen, or perhaps just picked up the color of the anomaly. His eyes, which had not shifted their focus from the wall, were watery and huge. Therese could see her shadow on them and turned to trace his gaze, which was locked to a sinuous purple vine. This was the same one she'd noticed before. The one sporting dozens of large, elegant thorns.

McArdle brought the dolly into position right behind Carver's back. They and Lissy quickly clicked open the straps on the base and laid them out to the side, ready to secure Carver if it became necessary. "Ready?" McArdle asked, and Lissy nodded. Each grabbed a shoulder.

Therese studied the thorns. What would it feel like, she wondered, to be pierced by one? Her right hand still held Carver's wrist. With her left, she reached as close to the anomaly as she dared. Then closer.

The moment she made contact, a current zapped through her arms, and Carver let out a long, high howl. He fell forward, despite McArdle and Lissy's straining arms.

"No!" he yelled. Therese was terrified but didn't let go of his wrist. "Please, don't take me away!"

"Carver!" Lissy screamed as her gloves lost purchase on his clothing.

"Dr. Blake, grab his legs! Come on!" McArdle yanked hard on the shoulder still in her grasp and Carver fell backward hard, making the dolly bounce against the stone floor with a loud bang. He kicked like a drowning man. Therese released his hand but her fumbling attempts to restrain his ankle failed when his leg shot out and kicked her hand. The pain was surprising and sharp, enough to make her worry something was broken.

Lissy and McArdle wrestled Carver back so the handle of the dolly framed his head. Lissy threw herself over his torso and McArdle worked quickly with the straps, clicking them together and pulling them tight. First at his chest, then at his waist. Finally Therese and her sister wrestled a leg each into submission, and McArdle tugged the final strap into place.

Carver hadn't stopped shouting, and all his shouts seemed directed at Therese. "You should know better!" he said between panting breaths. "It's shown me so much. I want to keep learning. You're a professor, you understand. Don't you?"

"I'm going to gag him," said McArdle, pulling a cord from some pocket on their suit. They stripped off his mask and tossed it behind them.

"I've been patient!" Carver spat. Veins in his neck stood out but softened as fighting the restraints got him nowhere. He dodged McArdle's cord while whimpering. "Please, just leave me here. I'm ready. I'm done. Don't take me away." McArdle finally got the gag between his teeth, and he went silent.

"You're not done," said Lissy. She pushed the dolly but Carver's boots caught on the floor, so she turned it and pulled instead. McArdle took up the lantern from the entrance, sending the shadows crashing around again.

Therese's hand hurt where Carver had kicked her. She undid the clasps and pulled off her glove to see if anything was broken or bleeding. Negative on both counts, but she would be swollen and sore in the morning. At the corner of her eye the thorns sparkled. They seemed to promise electricity, a pain that was sharp and sweet. She wasn't sure if that was preferable to her injury, but she leaned closer to the anomaly. It radiated warmth, which she felt even through her suit and mask. She held her injured hand over the light and rested her finger on the tip of one of the thorns.

She expected it to be as hard as the surrounding rock and as smooth as any stained glass she'd touched in museums or in bars, even though Carver's hands had shown that wasn't the case. Her finger sank into the anomaly but only by a few millimeters. It resisted gently, like the surface of a flan or a hard-boiled egg. Like flesh. She pushed in a bit harder. Pins and needles started in her fingertip and traced her arteries to her shoulder. It did ease the pain in her hand.

How thick was this surface layer? How far could she push? Would it stretch, tear, or eventually stop her? Would it let her go as easily as it had released Carver? Blood rushed in her ears. Crowds at rock concerts were quieter.

Beneath her finger, the purple vine wavered. Therese let out a yelp and pulled her finger away. It didn't fight her. The vine seemed still, now, but she could swear it had moved before. The thorns glinted. A trick of the light? Breath caught in her chest and wouldn't move. She pulled her hand away quickly, and the warmth left her.

"Professor? We're leaving," said McArdle.

Therese slipped her glove back on and snapped it into place, hoping no one noticed her transgression. Lissy pulled the dolly into the tunnel. Keeping their distance from Carver's kicking feet, McArdle and Therese followed.

Tsieh quickly turned the jumpship into a makeshift hospital room. He set up a saline drip and arranged a row of seats into the most awkward bed he'd ever seen. It wouldn't be comfortable but was probably better than the floor. He logged into the mainframe to disable the flight controls, only to find it already taken care of. McArdle must have done it before they left. They thought of everything. He missed them with a stab, then put on his suit to be ready when the others returned.

The sight of Carver nearly unconscious was a shock, but seeing him gagged was worse. McArdle told Tsieh about the trouble he gave them before they got him strapped down. They maneuvered the dolly through the entry to the jump. Tsieh and McArdle lifted Carver's prone form carefully and placed him on the bed. He lay there, still. Tsieh removed the gag before hooking him up to the saline. Otherwise he might vomit and choke.

Lissy stood over Carver, biting her lip. She spoke half-hearted insults, orders for him to get better, but Tsieh noticed the glassiness of her eyes and drew McArdle through the dock into the *Maris Stella* proper. He got a tour of some of the bruises Carver had inflicted while they stripped off their protective gear, then thanked them for disabling the jump. McArdle looked at him with wide eyes still ringed by the pressure marks of the goggles. Without another word they slipped away toward the cockpit. He would have followed, but he noticed Therese just emerging from the jump. She climbed into the ship, pulled off her mask, and leaned against the wall, breathing raggedly but saying nothing. Tsieh stepped closer to her. "How are you doing, Therese?"

Beneath her goggles, he could see her face was streaked with tears. She removed the goggles and wiped at them angrily. Tsieh was suddenly deeply embarrassed, both at and for Carver, and what this said about their crew. "I guess this doesn't happen on Earth digs," he said.

"Oh, it does." A laugh burst weakly from her lips. "This one time one of my colleagues crawled alone into a bottle of vodka because the nightlife was so boring."

"Was he okay?"

"Yeah, eventually. Went home early. Maybe being on these trips does stuff to people's heads, you know? Does it happen to you guys a lot? I mean, when we were in the cave, Carver said something so strange . . . "

"What did he say?"

She didn't get a chance to answer. Lissy emerged from the jumpship, sealed the entrance, and pulled off her mask. The lines etched on her face made her look twenty years older. "Well, this sucks," she said. "But at least he's sleeping. Thanks for putting in the line, Tsieh."

Tsieh said, "Sure. Are you okay, Boss?"

"Asshole probably just picked something up in the last port," Lissy replied, definitely not okay. She was starting to cry now and sniffed the tears back. Tsieh had seen Lissy cry before, but only with anger. She'd wept buckets after the last job went south, yelling and cursing for an hour straight. But the tears now seemed more of sadness and despair, and it unsettled him to see her famed swagger so completely spent. "How soon can we get to somewhere with a decent bar? And a hospital?"

"Not tonight." McArdle returned from the cockpit, their expression one of pure fury. "This ship isn't going anywhere. Someone messed with the controls and I can't even get her to turn over. We have life support and light and all that, but the drive system is completely offline. As are the comms, but we knew that. Probably connected."

"What do you mean, 'someone'?" Tsieh asked. "I was the only one here."

"And with all due respect, we didn't leave you alone long enough to do this level of damage." Tsieh was not consoled. "Carver was here the whole day, though. Maybe he wasn't shitting his brains out like you think he was, Boss."

"Don't," said Lissy. "Carver isn't lying about being sick, and he wouldn't hurt the ship."

"I would have said he *couldn't*," said McArdle. "Doesn't know the ship's ass from its elbow. Looks like I underestimated him. I need to spend the next few hours trying to get us off the ground, so when he does wake up, he's gonna hear about it from me. I don't care if he was delirious when he did it. Tsieh, would you join me in the engine room?"

"Sure." Tsieh couldn't ignore the rumble in his gut. Was it feeling sympathetic symptoms from Carver? Combined with both the ship and the boss seeming broken, it unnerved him. He kept searching McArdle's body language for the confidence they usually projected and found none there either.

The *Maris Stella* was home, but for the first time its corridors seemed dark, slick, and narrow, like the tunnels of the cave. He began to think that either place or both of them might be a trap.

Therese went to her quarters after Tsieh and McArdle left. She tried to gin up the energy to work, at least document everything that had happened, but she couldn't. Instead, she sat on her plastic cot and watched the tiny light on the emergency system blink on and off, on and off. She timed her breath to it, but that was too fast, so she shut her eyes and slowed down everything she could.

There was a knock at the door. Therese hesitated on the cot, her breathing jumbled again. Whoever was on the other side knocked again, harder. It was a sharp, hollow knock, not made with a fist. Therese was frightened, and ashamed of being frightened, and remained frozen. Not until the third knock did she get up and cross the room to open the door.

It slid aside to reveal Lissy in the lounge pants and shirt she usually wore to bed. The bottle of Irish cream in her hand had done the knocking. She carried no cups, and there was a bit of brown liquid dribbled onto her shirt front. She hefted the bottle to take another swig and said, "You don't need to lock your door. No one here is gonna hurt you." She stomped into the room and dropped like lead onto the cot. "Of course, I've locked plenty of the ship down for the night. Carver's sealed into the jump and we're sealed into the *Maris Stella*, in case he gets free. Nothing weird gets in. Or out." This was a joke, to judge from Lissy's Irish-cream-scented laugh.

Therese took the bottle from her sister's unresisting grip and sat beside her. "How much of this did you drink?" she asked, weighing it in her hands.

"I dunno. How much was left? Really wish I'd packed more. Or something stronger. I wonder if the colony site has booze? I mean, they were miners, right? What kind of self-respecting miner doesn't have booze on hand? Go ahead and take some. I didn't finish it. I don't think."

The bottle made a sloshing sound. Therese shrugged and took a sip, figuring the alcohol would put paid to any germs but not really caring either way. The sweetness clung to her tongue and burned her throat. She examined her sister closely. Lissy didn't seem particularly drunk, just . . . lost. Therese could relate. "McArdle making any progress on the engines?"

"Fuck if I know, they won't let me in. Which sucks. They and Tsieh can make out *after* the ship is in the air." Lissy held her hand out for the bottle, but Therese refused to hand it over.

"How's Carver doing?" she asked as gently as she could. "It must be really hard for you, seeing him like this."

"Like you care." The icy whisper needled into Therese's heart. "I guess you don't have to, though. It was nothing serious between us, anyway. Just fun. He didn't really like me all that much and I was only looking for a distraction."

"I don't believe that's true. And it's okay if you like him."

Lissy laughed again, raw and ugly. "You wanna know something true? I'll tell you something true. Carver never filed any of the documentation or permits for this expedition."

The bottle hung heavily in Therese's hand. She lowered it to the floor, away from Lissy, who didn't seem to notice.

"I know what you're thinking: he literally only has one job on this crew. File the paperwork, grease whatever needs greasing to do it. He's too good-looking to do much else. He never forgets, though. He's actually pretty dedicated to it."

"People screw up," was the only thing Therese could think to say.

"Yes, they do." Lissy tilted her head back and stared at the ceiling. "But it wasn't him. It was me. I told him to sit on the paperwork until I got you all here. That's why he never filed it." As Therese began working through what that could mean, Lissy said it aloud for her. "That means that with the comms down, we can't tell anyone we can't fly—can't ask for help. And no one would even think to come looking for us, because technically, legally, we're not supposed to be here." Lissy slumped forward, head in her hands. "And if they did come to rescue us, we would lose any proprietary claims we might have had otherwise, which kind of kills me, but it's a moot point now, I guess."

This was bad. Bad for all the reasons Lissy had listed, and a few more Therese could imagine. "It's okay," Therese said, putting a hand on Lissy's shoulder. "I'm sure you didn't mean for this to happen. On the next operation you won't make that mistake."

"You're not even listening!" Lissy shrugged off her sister's hand, stood up, and began to pace. "I'm saying we are *screwed*. And my crew and I, we needed this. I don't expect you to understand."

"I do understand. I have a lot riding on this too, you know."

Lissy's sigh was ragged and long. "Yeah, I know, you're gonna lose the publication. I'm really sorry, but at least you can go back to the university and . . . "

"I can't." Therese flopped onto her back, her spine cracking with the sudden movement. She stretched into it and it cracked again. "I didn't tell you. They wouldn't let me take a sabbatical. Publish or perish, and I haven't published enough. I figured if this was as big as you said, then I could get a monograph, hell, maybe an actual book out of it, and then I'd have something to show them. But it turns out anthropologists are thick enough on the ground that they didn't need me. When I told them I was going, they made as much clear. I don't have a job to go back to. I get to start from scratch, just like you, except now my department chair and my asshole ex-boyfriend are probably telling everyone I'm a huge flake. It's such an incestuous field, everybody's gonna know and everybody's gonna look at me sideways when I come back with nothing."

Therese rolled over to look at her sister. Lissy had stopped pacing and stood in the middle of the room facing the cot, tears streaming down her face, little paths reflecting the sick glow of the overhead lamp and the red blinking from the emergency sign. "Jesus, Therese, I wanted you to get something out of this. And maybe then you'd actually think what I do has any purpose, instead of treating me like a glorified garbage man."

"What?" Therese sat up so quickly she went lightheaded. "I don't think that!"

"You never stand up for me when Mom tells me to get a real job or go back to school. It's obvious you think I'm beneath you. You think we all are. Every time you come home you just sit in a corner and watch us like we're zoo animals. Don't think I don't see it."

"Hey!" Again, the dizziness. Therese clenched her fists against the bullshit her sister was spewing. "It's not my fault Mom nags you. She nags me too. Told me to finish my degree and brags about it but has no idea what I actually do, how hard it is, or how there's no fucking job security. For over fifteen years, I've been teaching people who don't care about something I used to love but right now cannot stand. You would know this if you ever bothered to ask me about it when I visit. But no, you and Mom are too busy with each other's business; you even have mutual friends. You brag about me but don't actually want to hear what I have to say. Every time I reach out, you're busy. Part of the reason I came out here was to learn more about what you do, but I dunno, maybe Mom was right the whole time."

"God, you are such a fucking snob."

The words in Therese's throat died and choked her. She refused to break eye contact with Lissy, to give her the satisfaction of winning. She refused to break that angry, brittle connection.

So Lissy did it for her. With a last glare at the bottle on the floor, too close to Therese to swipe up easily, she slapped the door control, stepped into the hallway, and without a single look back walked away into that harsh light.

The door took its time closing, and Therese was able to slip through behind Lissy without touching it. She followed Lissy to her quarters, maintaining a distance between the two of them, trying to keep her footfalls soft, though her shadow preceded her. Lissy didn't seem to notice it as she reached her own door and slammed the control. She slipped in and it closed behind her with a whisper. Therese stared dumbly for a moment before laying her hand on it.

She could knock.

Maybe it wasn't even locked.

But everything was too raw. What they both needed was sleep. Satisfied that Lissy was secure in her room, Therese went back to hers.

Tsieh watched McArdle contort their body into various channels and crevices in the engine room for over an hour. The problems with the ship ran so much deeper than the cockpit. Clanking, ratchets, the occasional snip of wire, and loud swearing from McArdle were the only sounds in the room. Tsieh handed them the tools they asked for and otherwise sat there, weighed down with thoughts and helpless to shift them. He felt worse than useless, because he couldn't think of anywhere outside the engine room that he'd be any help either.

"Tsieh? You still with me?" McArdle emerged from the latest panel they'd worked open. They blinked against the brighter overhead lights. Their eyes were probably tired from the effort of squinting, too—they always refused to wear magnifying or assistive goggles but instead relied on touch when they worked. That touch was superb. If he had any energy, he would long for it right about now. But he didn't, and he couldn't.

"I'm here. What do you need?" he asked.

McArdle didn't answer at first but studied him with the same intensity they used on the circuit boards of the guidance system. "Nothing," they said finally. "Tell me what's on your mind."

"Just wishing I could help you more with getting the ship in the air."

"You are helping," they said, selecting a wrench from the floor and reaching back almost casually to adjust something Tsieh couldn't even see. "You're handing me tools very carefully and slowly, which reduces the chance that I'll smash my own fingers."

Tsieh tried to laugh, but the pressure sinking over his chest wouldn't allow it. The smell of cooked wire rasped the inside of his nose and he sniffed, but that only made it worse. He grunted against the acrid taste in the back of his mouth, sniffed again, and sneezed. When he looked up, McArdle was buried in the heart of the engine again. Their voice came out muffled, filtered through the layers of tech that separated him from them, now as always. There was a screech and a snapping, and McArdle growled a long, "Fuuuuck."

"Talk to me," Tsieh said.

Another snap, another "Fuck!" and the smell of fire increased, sharp and chemical. McArdle wiggled out of the crawlspace, the rivets on their workpants scraping the floor. Eventually they got enough clearance to sit up, wire tool in hand, and look Tsieh in the face. "Carver really did a number on this."

"Easy," said Tsieh. "He's recovering from something, and we don't know he did this."

"Somebody did. No way any of this was an accident. Wires are cut so deep in the cockpit boards I almost lost fingerprints digging after them. Parts are missing that I don't have replacements for, because they don't usually fail, and I checked this ship over stem to stern before we came on this job. It was in perfect health, and now . . . " They choked up. "I don't know if I can get it airborne again. That bastard ruined my ship." McArdle's arm swept out in a sudden motion, and the tool they were holding clanged against a far wall before clattering on the floor. "And what's really pissing me off is I don't know how he knew how. If he was such a good mechanic, why did he always disappear when we needed repairs?" A loud crackle sounded behind a panel. McArdle's voice came back lower. "If he survives, by some miracle, I am going to kill him."

Tsieh didn't answer but shuffled over to McArdle and drew them close. They resisted, shoulders stiff, but finally relented and sank against him. He felt their shuddering breath and planted a kiss on their head. "You're right. We can't let him get away with this."

They looked up at him, eyes shiny. "Do you think we can make him buy me a new ship?"

He shrugged. "I was just going to back you up on beating the shit out of him."

McArdle chuckled and wiped their eyes. "Back to work, Tsieh."

"Would you even be happy with a new ship? The *Maris Stella* is yours." It was more than transport, more than a job. Tsieh had watched McArdle take care of this ship for years now. He knew what it meant to them: identity, freedom, home, and money. What would they be without it?

"There are other ships," they said, wiggling back into the crawlspace.

"You love this one."

"I don't love things." Another sparking noise.

"First lesson of the InDevCo evacuation," Tsieh said before they could.

"Damn right. Cut your losses, live to fight another day. Hand me back that wire tool, would you?"

He stretched out to pick up the tool they had flung away and placed it into their waiting hand, which disappeared along with the rest of them. He could not understand that casual dismissal.

He'd always stuck to things. To his schooling, his grad degree. When he joined up with the crew of the *Maris Stella*, it was his first taste of freedom. But it was never easy for him, the way it was for them. Now he was scrambling to grab onto something that would steady him in this nightmare they were caught in, but couldn't find anything. His legs cramped and he stood up, eyes burning with the smoke. "What would my dad think of me here, dying on this shit planet?"

"We're not dying. Where did I put the soldering iron?"

Tsieh located it after digging around in the toolbox and passed it to them. "I ever tell you what he said when I informed him I was joining you and Lissy's salvage operation? Something like, if I didn't finish my PhD, I'd end up crushed to death by a machine or working myself into an early grave."

"Yeah, well, no offense to your father?" McArdle's level of respect for the older Mr. Tsieh had always been clear by the tone of their voice, and this time was no different. "We've got Dr. Blake on this trip, and she's in as much trouble as the rest of us."

Therese. He'd almost forgotten about her. Maybe she could understand what was bugging him. He could check if she was up and dump all of this on her before it got between him and the person he owed everything to.

"Tsieh? You still there?"

"Yeah." He yawned. "I was thinking I'd go check on Carver, see if he woke up."

"What are you going to do if he did?" McArdle asked. Tsieh had no idea. They continued, "Seriously, just let him be until we get a doctor to look at him."

"Right. I think I should maybe go to the lab then."

"What?" McArdle's attention went back to whatever connection needed them now. For a long time Tsieh stood, listened, and watched. They didn't call for him. They probably didn't hear when he slid the toolbox across the floor to where they could reach it easily, tiptoed around where they were working, and let himself out of the door.

The lab. That was a joke at his expense. It was little more than a closet, a place for him to store his tapes and occasionally run spectrographic analysis to confirm the worth of the junk they were picking up.

Samples from the cave sat in a petri dish under a glass dome. He lifted the dome and looked closely at the little chunks of rock, which hadn't done anything spectacular since he'd taken them. They registered as completely normal, mostly iron, in all his tests. He brushed them into his palm. Closing his hand around them, he felt their jagged edges warm and melt beneath his bare skin, but when he opened his hand, they were the same as they had been. What could explain it? He squeezed them again, felt the phenomenon repeat. This time, when he observed them afterward, there seemed to be the faintest glow. He hurried to the wall and turned off the light to confirm. Nothing.

Now he was seeing things. He breathed in through his nose. The air in the lab was only as fresh as it got on board ship, but at least it didn't smell like an electrical experiment. By contrast, in fact, it reminded him of the cedarish scent of the cave.

He dropped the chunks back into their dish, where they clattered like dice, and replaced the dome. He'd forgotten more about organic chemistry than anyone on the ship ever knew, but it was forgotten nonetheless. With comms down, he couldn't access his usual reference materials. He was no closer to identifying what the anomaly was, or why Carver was so drawn to it. He sat spinning in the lab chair, a rickety steel number he'd claimed on an early job and which McArdle had personally welded to the floor so it wouldn't fall over if the artificial grav glitched. Once he was good and dizzy he stopped by slipping his leg between the lower rungs. The pain cleared his head. He stood and stumbled out of the lab to the jump dock, brushing invisible dirt off his hands as he did so.

The door to the jumpship had no window. There was no way to see in except to open it, which would violate Lissy's orders and get her good and pissed at him, plus he'd probably need to put his containment suit on, and he wasn't in the mood. He considered knocking at Therese's door. McArdle wouldn't mind, they weren't a suspicious type, but still it didn't feel like a good idea. He had no good ideas at all.

He looked longingly down the hall to where the main door of the ship lay. There was no going outside either. What would he do? Nothing. He was nothing here and worth nothing. He went to his room and collapsed on his cot, worry drilling him into sleep.

DAY THREE

A sharp pain in her gut woke Therese early the next morning. She shoved herself out of bed and ran to the toilet, grateful for the private bathroom in her quarters. Afterward the pain was gone, or at least duller, but she was unsteady on her feet. She leaned against the wall to wait for the room to stop spinning and tasted the sticky residue of Irish cream turned sour, coating her mouth and teeth. "Lissy!" she said, startling herself with a rush of memories. She didn't trust her balance enough to get dressed, but she had to check on her sister. Her shorts and shirt would have to do.

The light from the hall sliced into her vision. She squeezed her eyes shut, her pulse beating against her temples, and swallowed against another wave of nausea. It receded but didn't disappear. Now there were sounds in her ears, almost an itch. A rhythm growing louder and louder, then fading, stopping. She opened her eyes to see McArdle a few paces down the hall. She called the pilot's name, at which they turned and came to stand in front of her. "You look like hell," said Therese.

McArdle's eyes were set in deep, bleak hollows. Their curls stuck to one side of their head, and their clothes were covered in dust and streaked with black. Odors of ozone, carbon, and sweat came off their person in waves. "None of us are winning any beauty contests this morning, Professor. Where's your sister?"

"I was gonna go get her."

"Great. We'll go together."

Together meant that McArdle jogged while Therese staggered behind on a metal floor that grew colder against her bare feet with every step. At the door McArdle knocked once, then again. They put their ear against it and listened. "Yeah, we don't have time for this," they said. They pushed the outer door control ten times in rapid succession, then pulled a tool from their pocket and removed the control panel entirely. One stab into the mess of wires and chips and the door slid open, like it had only been waiting to be asked roughly.

The room was empty. McArdle tossed the bedsheets, as if Lissy might be hiding in the polyester pile. Therese thought she heard her sister's voice nearby and inspected the bathroom, which was clean and dry. If Lissy had been sick, there was no evidence. "She's not here," Therese said, but McArdle was already halfway out the door. "Where are you going?"

Further observation yielded the obvious answer. It was time to check on Carver.

Tsieh was already by the jump entrance, wearing his suit. The goggles and mask hid his face, but his posture was that of a man who hadn't slept last night. Therese felt guilty for the sleep she did get and was immediately angry at so useless an emotion.

"Boss is gone," McArdle announced to Tsieh. "Not in her room, not anywhere else."

"Where did she go?" he asked.

Therese knew. She was sure the others could guess.

"Open it up, Tsieh," said McArdle.

"Don't you want your suit?" he asked, holding out the folded pile of gear and a box of gloves.

McArdle swore. "We were holed up in the same ship, breathing the same air for days, Tsieh. Let's just see if he's alive so we can plan our next move." But Tsieh only stood defiant in front of the entrance. Eventually McArdle wrested themself into goggles, a mask, and a pair of gloves, but that was clearly as far as they would go. They sidled around Tsieh and into the jump. He dropped the rest of the gear. As if he'd just noticed Therese, he said, "Stay here. We'll be a second."

That suited her fine. He stepped around the gear on the floor and into the connection to the jump. She heard the outer door's pneumatic wheeze as it shut, and the same, more muffled sound from the inner one. And then she heard a cry from Carver that froze her blood. Stopping only to gather gloves, she followed Tsieh.

The smells hit her first. The rubber of the gloves, the close air of a sickroom with inadequate ventilation. She clapped her hand to her mouth and nose. She hadn't grabbed a mask. She should leave immediately. But she couldn't. "I heard him scream," she said weakly between her fingers.

"Nobody's screaming," said McArdle.

Carver lay as they had left him, a thin blanket draped over his form. Tsieh was nudging him, shaking him, but he didn't respond. McArdle called his name, their fingers probing his neck for a pulse. "I can't find it," they said.

"Lemme check the line," said Tsieh. He fished under the blanket for Carver's arm and pulled it free. He gave a loud cry and dropped the limb.

Carver's arm at the shoulder was an ashen color, matching his face. But toward the elbow the skin took on a sheen like rainbows on the surface of an oil slick or scales of a diseased snake. By the wrist, it shone in the weak artificial light of the jump. His fingers, however, had turned the black and green of rotting vegetation, and stretched to twice their length. Released from Tsieh's grip, Carver's arm flopped onto the cot and then hung over the edge. The ends of his blackened fingers dropped off and landed on the floor with a dull splat.

The three of them stood in shocked silence. Tsieh stood stupidly, holding the needle with trembling fingers. McArdle was steady as ever, not even their curls moving as they gripped the edge of the blanket and pulled it back from Carver's body. Now they could see that his other hand was likewise maimed, and a hint of the rainbow glow peeked through the neck hole of his shirt. Exposed to the cold, Carver's body pulled in on itself, and his eyes snapped open. They were blank and unseeing, smears of incandescence with no life behind them. When he drew in a breath and screamed, it was no human sound.

"Out. Now!" McArdle yelled. Therese did not need the order. She cowered just outside the inner door until McArdle emerged. In the connecting area they stripped off their gloves and goggles and mask and left them in a pile before stepping fully back into the *Maris Stella*. Therese followed, with Tsieh close behind. McArdle slammed the hatch button with such force the plastic cracked, scratching their hand. "Galley," they said, wincing over the tiny line of blood. "We're gonna need coffee."

Tsieh did not obey. Not at first.

First he ducked into the decon shower and let the water sluice over him until it ran cold. The scene played itself in a loop no matter how hard he shut his eyes or how loud he hummed or how hard the shower pelted him. Carver's fingers falling off. His scream.

When he was dressed and finally made it to the galley, he found Therese assembling a pile of food on the table while McArdle emptied what looked like a triple batch of coffee into three insulated bottles lined up beside the press. They screwed the lids on, one at a time, and held one out to Therese. The professor looked lost and waved it away.

"Drink it or don't, but it's the last we're going to get for a while," McArdle said. Therese took the bottle, as did Tsieh when McArdle handed him his. "Eat something. Eat a lot. We pack the rest." There was no room to argue, no better idea. Therese collapsed into a chair, put her bottle on the table, and bit into the pastry she'd unwrapped. Tsieh followed suit.

"Okay, this is where it sits," McArdle began. "The ship is fucked. I can't get it airborne. We're lucky we have life support and hot water."

Therese said, "I'm sure you did your best with it."

McArdle tagged her with a pointed glare. "I never do anything else."

"I'm so sorry," Tsieh offered.

"Save the condolences. We have bigger problems. Our fearless leader is missing. We're grounded. And Carver is . . . he's gone. We need to grab the bug-out bags and leave."

"We can't leave Carver," Therese said through a mouthful of crumbs. "Lissy wouldn't leave one of us behind."

"That's exactly what Lissy's done, if you haven't noticed." McArdle took a deep breath and a bite of the toast in front of them, chasing it with a gulp of coffee. "And Carver's not one of us anymore. I don't know what he is. The fact is, we can't do anything about it. So we're going to do what we can, which is pack and get the hell off the ship."

"Okay." Tsieh wiped his mouth. The food was like shredded paper on his tongue. He considered the coffee, decided against it. "I'll get the dolly. I didn't put my stuff back on it."

"No." McArdle shook their head solemnly. "Nothing we can't carry, because we're going over the ridge to the miners' site." Therese stopped chewing to gape. "Mouths closed, guys. This is what has to happen. There are supplies and parts there.

A safe place to sleep. And ships that might work. It's our best bet."

"That's a hell of a climb, McArdle." Tsieh leaned back to do the calculations in his head. "Plus a couple klicks to the site itself."

"I know. The ridge isn't going to be that bad. I saw some sort of track when I passed over it in the jump. Looks climbable. It'll just be a hike. Dr. Blake, is it something you can handle?"

"I'm pretty sure I could handle it, if it came to that." Therese was absently dry-washing her hands. Tsieh found the movement fascinating. "But finding Lissy should be a priority. I'm worried about her."

"I'm more worried about us," said McArdle.

"Hang on," Tsieh replied. "You're not really suggesting we abandon her. I mean, really, not even look for her? What if she needs help? We don't know where she is."

"We know where she is," said Therese. "She went to the cave, like Carver did."

"Yeah." McArdle nodded. "Not looking to do that again."

"Are you cutting your losses?" Tsieh's hands were trembling again. He decided it was from anger and not fear because that was easier.

"She could still need us. And the cave's on the way to the ridge," Therese joined. "It won't take long to find her. Please."

McArdle's face settled into stone. "No," they said. "We're not going back into that cave for anything. Eat as much food as you can hold, and visit the head, because I don't know when we'll see the next one. Then grab your stuff."

By the time they were ready to leave, huge bags strapped to their backs, wearing masks and gloves but no complete suits because damn it, there just wasn't time, the sun had completed about a third of its march across the sky. McArdle did not relish the idea of getting caught outside in the dark. Everyone carried a lantern and extra oxygen for the climb. A bottle of surplus coffee added weight to each person's pack, but not a one had objected.

The very metal and plastic of the *Maris Stella* tugged at their heart as McArdle stepped through the hatch for the last time. They'd taken as much time as they could, probably more than was wise, visiting the engine room to look for salvageable parts, confirm the absolute disaster condition of the ship's heart, and whisper their apologies and farewells. The galley, where they'd cooked, the cockpit that was their domain—they left a final blessing breath in each place. Only the jump dock received no such attention. Sentiment, perhaps, but also practicality. Lost causes would be left behind.

Outside on the sand, Tsieh helped them seal up the ship. He placed his hands on their shoulder, turning the tug in their heart into a sharp pain. They resented his trying to force some sort of emotional outburst from them and clenched their jaw against it. "Do you need more time?" Tsieh asked, his lips close to their ear.

They stood straight and faced the direction of the cave. "Taken too much already. Other ships, Tsieh. It'll be fine. Now." They held a hand over their eyes and scanned the ground before them, and the horizon. The black hole of the cave was visible from here, but they were surveying the ridge near it. A feature of the wind-blasted rock stood out, something they hadn't quite seen before. McArdle stepped forward, hand still raised. Then they smiled. Good news at last.

They gestured Tsieh closer to point out what they'd found, when the view was interrupted by movement many yards ahead. "Oh, great."

"What's the problem?" Tsieh asked, confused.

"Didn't know the professor could move that fast."

Therese had gotten a head start. A dust cloud kicked up cartoonishly in her wake as she stalked away.

"Why didn't she wait for us?" Tsieh asked. "Oh. She's going to find Lissy."

"Let her. Come on, Tsieh, we're burning daylight."

He backed away from them, toward the ridge. "I can't," was all he said before turning and jogging to catch up with the receding figure of Therese ahead of him.

McArdle shifted their pack off their back to the ground. Fishing around in a pocket they retrieved a coiled length of cord. "Wait for me," they called.

Therese couldn't wait for the others. The path was clear, even without Lissy's barefoot tracks in the sand. It was a pull that started in her palms and crept up her arms to her heart. Her sister was in the cave. Lissy had gotten ahead of her and left her behind. It was unforgivable. She would make it right.

She heard the shouts behind her and walked faster. On the

rock ledges and the scraggly trees that scratched their presence against the dusty sky, the rooks sat placidly and watched her, their leathery wings reflecting light. She took a moment to admire them, then started to run.

Inside the cave, all was at last cool, calm, and subdued. She followed the tunnel, brushing the smooth, glassy surfaces of the walls. The sensation was too dull, so she pulled off her gloves. A soft glow replaced the fading light from the tunnel entrance and she noticed with appreciation that it came from the tips of her fingers.

The ceiling dropped low, familiar and welcoming, but the burden she was carrying would not allow her to pass easily. She shrugged it off and it hit the floor with a clunk. After ducking under the dip in the ceiling, she reached behind to pull the straps and wedge the pack in the space, blocking the path.

One turn became another until she stood again in that temple, the anomaly with all its life and beauty beckoning her, and Lissy waiting.

Her sister stood at attention before the anomaly, hands reaching forward in an attitude of prayer or awe. She wore nothing but her sleep clothes. Her fingers, resting on the anomaly, had just begun to dent its surface. "Hello, big sister. I've been waiting for you."

Therese slipped her mask off and tossed it away. There would be no barriers between them anymore. They were together, where they belonged. She approached her sister quietly, reverently, like she was attending a birth. She rested her hands on Lissy's shoulders. "I'm here now."

Lissy's fingers sank into the glowing surface by an inch or

two. The tips disappeared beneath the color and light. It looked so inviting, like the touch pools at the aquarium where in their younger days they had spent hours brushing anemones and chasing tiny fish. The anomaly's flora and fauna moved too—they moved! No mistake about that now. The branches slid and twisted around each other. The insects formed their own spirals. Where the anomaly had been a random riot of hues and forms before, it now had a focus: Lissy's hands.

"The others are behind me," Therese said. "They'll try to help."

The smile Lissy turned to her was warm and genuine, the kind Therese had seldom seen on her face before. "Tell them I'm sorry. McArdle especially. They've saved my life a couple of times, and running out this morning without telling them was a shitty way to thank them."

"You can thank them yourself, when they join us," Therese said.

"I will, later, if I remember. I honestly don't know what I'm going to be later, when we're all together, so maybe I won't? I don't know. Do you see, T? Do you see how I'm growing?"

Lissy's fingers were not her fingers anymore. Her hands were splitting down the middle, the fingers stretching into tendrils like Carver's, only bright and alive with the rest of the wall. A thumb separated itself and turned into a winged creature. Another fingertip became a fly that swam through the anomaly before coming to rest on a flower. The light and movement reflected in Lissy's eyes as she stared at the display with a look of absolute bliss and satisfaction. Color from the wall spread like jam over the flesh of Lissy's bare arms. A creeping ring of it shone around her throat. Therese looked again at the tips of her own fingers, her luminous nails and flesh. They were stinging now, burning, and she knew the only way to soothe them was to follow her sister in.

Lissy sighed as she stepped forward, arms covered and transformed to her elbows. Her eyes were bulging, stretching toward the anomaly like molten glass. "Thank you for being here with me. Not just now, not just on this job, but always and forever. You are so smart and so brave and I wouldn't be here without you. I love you, big sister."

The slightest fear brushed Therese's heart as she heard these words. She'd waited so long, and now the time was so short. Tears sparkled on her sister's skin. Distantly, she heard sounds that might have been McArdle and Tsieh in the tunnels. She imagined them shoving at the obstacle she'd left for them. It would be too late, now.

Lissy's brow touched the anomaly. Her head followed, and it was over quickly after that. The light spread through her entire body, transforming her into a riot of color and glassy radiance. Her torso became a bouquet of anemones and seaweed spreading out along the cave wall. Her flimsy clothing turned to the faintest ash upon contact. One bare foot stepped in, then the other, becoming a bright butterfly spreading jewel wings amid the blooms. Then nothing remained but the ache in Therese's fingers where the contact had broken. She sank to her knees and watched the anomaly slow in its movement, growing static in the syrup of the glass. It was hardening but never truly solid. She reached for it, rising up to join her sister and who knows how many people gone before.

Heaving the professor's pack out of their way had taken more strength than McArdle counted on. They tore through the remaining length of the tunnel, Tsieh right beside, and arrived out of breath just in time to see the boss swallowed up by the wall. There was nothing of her left behind. They stood frozen at the mouth of the cave and bleated a frantic little scream before scrambling to seize Therese under her arms and pull her away. Tsieh moved quietly and instinctively and grabbed her ankles. Together they maneuvered Therese as far from the anomaly as possible and propped her against the far wall.

It wasn't like it had been with Carver. When he realized what they were doing he had fought, literally kicking and screaming. The professor was like overcooked pasta, offering no resistance and making no noise. For some reason McArdle found this scarier. They dropped their pack to the ground, leaned against the wall, and slid down next to Therese, not taking their eyes off her the whole time. She was still, so still that McArdle wondered if she might be dead, which would be another tragedy but would simplify what came next, and that wasn't something they could ignore.

Therese reached her arm out to Tsieh, who stepped aside and scuttled next to McArdle against the wall. She raised her other arm, and her body leaned to follow, clearly pointing to the anomaly. McArdle grabbed her nearest shoulder and pulled her back to the wall. The process started again a few moments later.

"What are you doing?" Tsieh asked as they pulled the coil of rope from their pocket and shook it loose.

"Help me," McArdle said.

With Tsieh propping up an unresisting Therese, they wound the rope around her shoulders, looping it with care when they got to her arms. The rope slipped from Tsieh's gloves once, twice, and he handed the ends to McArdle so he could remove his gloves for a better grip. Once his hands were free he finished the task, and together they laid Therese on the floor. McArdle rolled her gently to face away from the anomaly. Even away from the light, her eyes sparkled. It was unnerving.

McArdle scraped themself off the floor, dusting off their gloves and pants, backing away from the professor. They fumbled for the small flashlight they kept on their belt and turned it on, the acid light dimming the unnatural glow from the wall and giving them a chance to think. And grab the closest bottle of coffee. The brew had cooled a bit but was still delicious. They handed it to Tsieh, who didn't drink but set it on the floor.

"Okay, Tsieh," they said. "We can't stay in the cave. The professor isn't in any shape to walk, and I don't think untying her would be a good idea. We leave her here, she'll follow Lissy . . ." McArdle choked. There was grief, but no time. A quiet thump came from the bundle that was Therese, as she lifted her head and set it down. "Can you help me carry her to the other site?"

"No," Tsieh said.

"That's it, just no?" McArdle finally turned to face him, waiting for the usual evidence and logic, but nothing came. Tsieh stared at his palms. "I'll get her shoulders, you get her feet. It'll be awkward but we can do it."

"I'm not sure it's a good idea," he said, still not looking up.

"I don't know if I can get over the ridge." Each word he spoke was halting, stiff, a struggle. McArdle felt their blood run cold when he finally met their eyes. He held out his palms to them and said, "I don't know that it will let me."

The light from the flashlight began to waver, to shake in McArdle's trembling hand, and they clicked it off. Once it was dim again, they could see the iridescent spots, one in the center of each of his palms. They grabbed for his wrist, intending to wipe away the offending blotches with their glove, but he avoided them deftly and resumed staring.

"You shouldn't come any closer to me, or to Therese, and certainly stay away from the anomaly." His voice was normal now, the soft, reasonable one he used in the lab or when explaining some incredible concept over dinner. Not patronizing, just matter-of-fact and so easy to listen to, McArdle could do it all day. "I don't know how, but it appears to be contagious."

"Not you," said McArdle.

"Seems so." He flexed his fingers. Now they glinted like mica. "It doesn't hurt, but there's definitely a feeling. A tug. It eases if I go closer." He didn't turn toward it, though, closing his hands into fists with visible effort. "And now it burns, just a little. It's strange."

McArdle punched his shoulder. Hard. He grunted at the impact, but said nothing. McArdle said, "Stop it. We're getting out of here, now. We'll take the professor, or not, but we're getting you as far away as possible."

"I'm not sure I can climb. Remember that article you showed me about toxoplasmosis? When I wanted a cat? How the parasite makes insects want to be eaten?" Tsieh asked.

"Yeah, I remember."

"If you try to take Therese, if you take me, we'll only hold you back. That's not fair. Go without me."

"Bullshit. We started this together, and that's how we'll finish it."

He looked at them with something approaching awe. "I want to tell you to come with me instead, but that wouldn't be me talking. And I don't want that. I want you to escape, and live, and never look back." He sank to his knees, breathing labored. "I never completed my analysis. Another thing I failed to finish." He looked up at them, his hazel eyes flecked with glittering motes of color.

McArdle had never hated color so much in their life. "You think I'm going to leave you behind to die? Look at me!" McArdle tore off their mask, knelt before him, and took his shoulders in their hands.

"I'm not sure it'd be dying." His voice was wistful now, his head turning to the anomaly. "I think it's like going home."

"How?" They pulled his head back as softly as possible. They took his hand, and now he didn't resist. "What am I going to do without you? Who's going to teach me more than anyone else knows about the universe? Who's going to set up the lab in my new ship? Who's going to help me engineer a new coffee press?" Each question sounded dumber than the last, but they kept on. "Who's going to help me pick a new ship and make it our home? Not my ship, not the crew's, but ours? I can't do that without my heart there with me, damn it!"

Tsieh rested his forehead against theirs. McArdle slipped his mask off, let it hang around his neck, and he didn't fight them.

His breath smelled of toothpaste. What would mornings be without that smell? They put a hand behind his head and pulled him closer. Kissed lips that didn't respond.

"I'm sorry, McArdle." He tried to pull away. They wouldn't let him. "The anomaly. Whatever it is, it wants me."

"I want you more." Another kiss, as if they could press into his very skin a reminder that they were human together. "And I'm going to fight for you like it never could. I love you, Tsieh."

His face was wet, they were both crying now. But he was kissing them back, holding them close, and the tears were gratitude that rained onto their clothes and sparkled for a moment before being absorbed. But they were still here, both of them, clinging to each other for love and life.

After they finally broke the embrace, after McArdle wiped Tsieh's eyes, which had gone back to a uniform hazel, Tsieh asked, "Can we get a cat?"

Therese was silent but not unaware.

Watching her sister disappear into the anomaly sparked such sadness, envy, and joy in her that the most prudent course seemed simply to sit and feel for a while. She allowed herself to be restrained, turned, ignored. One last time she would play the role she had so often assumed: the one no one noticed or spoke to but who observed everything around her. In her position against the curve of the wall, all the sounds in the cave flowed directly to her ears, loud against the anomaly's background hum: voices of colonists and cultists, Lissy's now among them.

Therese couldn't make out everything they said, but she heard enough to know patience would be rewarded.

The conversation between her two former crewmates made her heart sting, but it was a pleasant sting. She heard the resignation in Tsieh's voice, the passion in McArdle's, how the latter won him over. Their happiness was worth waiting a little longer for them to join her, and Lissy, and the others. But they might try to take her from this cave, and that was unacceptable. She began rocking back and forth on the cave floor. She expected the ropes would hurt as she pressed them between the rock and her flesh, but perhaps she had lost circulation. Or her circulation had become something else entirely. She rolled her body once and stopped, belly down, chin resting ridiculously on the ground. Her hands were secured behind her, but that was not a problem. She twisted and sweat pricked her skin. With a breath in she reached, stretched with her right hand, and soon saw her fingers beside her head. A few more moments, and the fingers of her left hand joined them. Together they flattened, lined up like pawns on a chessboard, and pushed until she was rolling again.

The sobs and laughter of Tsieh and McArdle's embrace choked to a stone silence. Therese didn't look at them. Their expressions would ruin this moment, so she concentrated on winding her arms around her body to roll herself over again. Scraping and cries moved toward her, then away, and then they sounded in the tunnel outside. Her plan had worked. They'd fled what she was becoming. For now.

She bore them no ill will for binding her or abandoning her. Before this change her thoughts would have been a fog of pain and grief, but now she saw with absolute clarity. These knots were not going to hold her back. Nothing was going to hold or contain her ever again: not her job, not Dave, not her mother's expectations, and certainly not this thin, simple cord.

Another roll brought her within a meter of the anomaly. One more brought her close enough to touch it. The ropes shifted as her entire body lengthened. Her fingers, still in formation, slid over every bump and scrape in the rock floor, increasing in speed up the wall. When they finally sank into the glowing surface, Therese sighed with contentment and pleasure. She marveled at the comfort and the beautiful flowers that already grew from her body. Her hand was a vine, digits sharp and shiny. Finally, the meek professor had thorns. A stem roped from her arms and entwined with the others. She recognized the unique color of Lissy's growth and wept with joy to see that they were finally working together to create something beautiful.

She pushed in further and bees buzzed from her.

Her limbs easily slipped the ropes once they had stretched enough. Her body slithered like a serpent as it fed into the anomaly. She remembered the rook's breakfast, two days and forever ago, life turned into abstract art by their predations. Was their hard work appreciated by their prey?

The voices were clearer now. Everyone who had ever left the world behind and joined in, the voices as one sounding something like love. Distantly, she felt Tsieh. She was connected to him through the indelible sparks on his palms. He and McArdle were halfway over the ridge by now, and with every step his light grew dimmer. They would find their ship, find their way off planet, but the light would never fade completely. Someday, he would return. And he would bring others.

Her eyes got ahead of her face, reaching across time and space of their own accord. She imagined every strand of her hair coming to life, Medusa's snakes bursting with every hue imaginable.

Her stalk eyes touched the anomaly at last. And it was glorious.

ACKNOWLEDGMENTS

I would like to thank Lanternfish Press for their support of this book, especially Christine Neulieb for her sharp editorial eye and Feliza Casano for the hustle.

Thanks also to Isabelle Leo Smith, for their sensitive reading of the manuscripts. Any remaining blunders are mine.

The South Shore Scribes have my gratitude for listening to my story and giving me feedback and confidence.

Finally, to my husband and kids, thank you for indulging my trips to the Museum of Fine Arts, reading my rough drafts, and helping me work out some of the details of this story. I love you!

ABOUT THE AUTHOR

JESSICA LÉVAI has loved stories and storytellers her whole life. After a double major in history and mathematics, a PhD in Egyptology, and eight years of the adjunct shuffle, she devoted herself to writing full-time. You can find her work at *Strange Horizons, Cossmass Infinities,* and *Reactor Magazine.* Her first novella, *The Night Library of Sternendach: A Vampire Opera in Verse*, won the Lord Ruthven Award for Fiction. Check out her website, JessicaLevai.com, for links and more.